Praise for the *New York Times* bestselling I

DEMON STORM

"..non-stop tense action, filled with twists, betrayals, danger, and a beautiful sensual romance. As always with Dianna Love, I was on the edge of my seat, unable to pull myself away." ~~Barb, The Reading Cafe

"...nonstop adventures overflowing with danger and heartfelt emotions. DEMON STORM leaves you breathless on countless occasions." ~~Amelia Richard, SingleTitles

"There is so much action in this book I feel like I've burned calories just reading it." ~~D Antonio, Goodreads

RISE OF THE GRYPHON

"...It's been a very long time since I've felt this passionate about getting the next installment in a series. Even J. K. Rowling's Harry Potter books. It's a story you don't want to end and when it does, you can't help but scream out 'No! NO THEY DID NOT JUST DO THIS TO ME!! NO!!!!'" ~~Bryonna Nobles, Demons, Dreams and Dragon Wings

"...shocking developments and a whopper of an ending... and I may have exclaimed aloud more than once...Bottom line: I really kind of loved it." ~~Jen, Amazon Top 500 Reviewer

THE CURSE

"The Beladors series is beloved and intricate. It's surprising that such a diverse and incredible world has only three books out." ~~Jessie Potts, USA Today, Happy Ever After

"If you're looking for a series with an epic scope and intricate, bold characters, look no further than the Belador series...This new addition provides all the action and intrigue that readers have come to expect...a series to be savored by urban fantasy and paranormal romance fans alike." ~~Bridget, The Romance Reviews

ALTERANT

"There are SO many things in this series that I want to learn more about; there's no way I could list them all... have me on tenterhooks waiting for the third BELADOR book. As Evalle would say, 'Bring it on.'" ~~Lily, Romance Junkies Reviews

"An incredible heart-jolting roller-coaster ride...An action- packed adventure with an engrossing story line and characters you will grow to love." ~~ Mother/Gamer/Writer

BLOOD TRINITY

"BLOOD TRINITY is an ingenious urban fantasy with imaginative magical scenarios, characters who grab your every thought and more than a few unpredictable turns ... The meticulous storyline of Book One in the Belador series will enthrall you during every compellingly entertaining scene." ~~Amelia Richard, Single Titles

"BLOOD TRINITY is a fantastic start to a new Urban Fantasy series. The VIPER organization and the world built ... are intriguing, but the characters populating that world are irresistible. I am finding it difficult to wait for the next book to find out what happens next in their lives." ~~Diana Trodahl, Fresh Fiction

TRISTAN'S ESCAPE

THE BELADOR SERIES

NEW YORK TIMES **BESTSELLING AUTHOR**

DIANNA LOVE

TRISTAN'S ESCAPE:
Novella from the Belador urban fantasy world

This NOVELLA timeline falls between Witchlock and Rogue Belador (April 2016). I hope you enjoy Tristan's story ... and there's a very short story at the end as a bonus. The character in that story is one of my favorites.

ACKNOWLEDGMENTS

As always, I have a wonderful team around me. I'd like to think Cassondra Murray, Judy Carney, Joyce Ann McLaughlin, Steve Doyle, Kim Huther and all the wonderful readers who are the reason I write every day. A thank you also to Kim Killion, who creates great covers for me, and Jennifer Jakes who passes her formatting wand over my pages.

Thanks also to the Dianna Love Street Team Facebook group page (all readers are invited) where we throw all the rules out the window. Thanks to Candi Fox for keeping us from falling into utter chaos.

No book happens without the love and support of my husband Karl, and our opinionated saltwater fish.

CHAPTER 1

Swooping into an approach pattern over Treoir Island, Tristan spread his gryphon wings for descent before he ran out of power and crashed.

He'd flown two double shifts of surveillance flights in the past two days. Exhaustion pushed him to hurry up and get done, but rushing could be hazardous. He'd prefer a nice, smooth landing to slamming into the angry waves dousing boulders below the bluffs. Sunlight faded as the only sign of a day ending. A mist over the Irish Sea hid this realm from the other worlds.

Visitors were not welcome.

The goddess Macha ruled this domain that was inhabited by her warrior queen and Treoir castle minions.

Plus eight unhappy gryphons.

Including the one now in human form, waiting at Tristan's private landing spot. Just seeing him there was a bad sign.

What was up with Bernie?

That skinny guy could shift whenever he wanted in this place. When he did, he turned into a badass, silver-gray gryphon that rose ten feet in height. On the other hand, Bernie was on the weak side as a human and panicked easily.

Like now. He was wringing his hands.

He wouldn't be here about a rift among the gryphons. They were aggressive beasts by nature. Blood flowed sometimes, but Tristan didn't care as long as his sister wasn't in the middle of any squabble. Petrina was not currently on Treoir Island.

That narrowed the potential disasters to one serious enough to send Bernie here. Macha.

Shit, if the goddess bitch called a meeting of all the gryphons right now, Petrina would end up screwed four ways.

Tristan picked up speed and slid into a fast landing. The second his giant lion paws hit solid ground he stomped forward. Gryphons were a majestic mix of eagle head and upper body atop a lion-shaped lower half, complete with a tail.

Since none of them could speak in this form, Tristan called out telepathically to Bernie. *What the hell is going on?*

Bernie lifted his finger to his lips and shook his head.

He didn't want to use telepathy?

That just reinforced Tristan's bad feeling. Macha might be listening for telepathic chatter.

No telepathy meant Tristan had to shift back into his human form here, where he had no spare clothes. Unlike the other gryphons, he *could* majik up a pair of jeans—sometimes—but that would further drain what was left of his power reserve.

Yep, Bernie showing up now was bad news, especially since the guy wanted Tristan rested enough to take him to Atlanta in three days. That would be Tristan's last secret teleportation trip for the holidays, thank the miserable gods. Had Macha figured out Tristan's secret transport service? Doubtful, since Tristan hadn't been turned into a flying ball of flame.

Macha was too arrogant to imagine anyone breaking her rules.

Lack of imagination had been the downfall of others who'd underestimated Tristan.

The goddess had a lot to learn about his gifts. To be honest, he did, too, but he definitely had a few tricks up his sleeve.

Or under his feathers, as it were.

Tristan called up his power to change back into human form, and groaned. With a few hours rest, this wouldn't take so long, but he'd been flying double shifts for weeks to keep the Treoir guards from getting suspicious about where he'd been spending his time off. Muscle and bone drew tight, changing shape as his giant wings shrank. He twisted and sucked down into a six-foot-two man. Sweat poured off his forehead and ran down his neck by the time he'd finished.

"Sorry, Tristan."

Cool air brushed his naked skin, but Tristan had lived naked most of four years during an imprisonment, so this was minor. "This better be good."

Bernie's bright green eyes filled with anxiety. "It's not. Wait. No.

I mean, this *is* important, but not good. What I'm, uh, just trying to say–"

Tristan rolled his shoulders, stretching the tight muscles. He waved his hand in a circular motion. "I've got it. Just tell me why you're here so I can get a damn shower and go to bed."

"Oh, sorry." Bernie wrung his hands again. "Evalle's coming here in two days."

Tristan did pause at that.

Technically, Evalle lead the gryphons, because the most powerful beast ruled their pack and she'd killed the deadliest gryphon in the pack when he'd attacked her during a battle. The gryphons were all half-blood Beladors also known as Alterants and, for now, they had to stay on Treoir to guard the island and castle. Evalle generally stayed in the human world unless Macha called her in, due to Evalle's unique position of being the gryphon liaison.

Some days Tristan hated the Belador part of his DNA.

But he cared even less for the other half.

Beladors were descended from ancient warriors who had once been badasses running around killing everything, especially their enemies. In particular, they'd targeted a group following a Hindu god. That shit stopped when Macha struck a deal with the Hindu god, where she'd keep her warriors under control and he'd deal with his.

The goddess gave Beladors one option. Swear to a code of honor or die. Simple enough, but now they had to fight the Medb coven of warlocks and witches, their greatest enemy, with their hands tied most of the time.

Medb blood ran through Tristan's body, too, but he'd just as soon let the Beladors and Medb have at each other. He would ignore both camps altogether if it didn't mean leaving his foster sister and the other gryphons to face the future alone.

Rubbing the sore muscles in his neck, Tristan started thinking out loud. "Evalle's visit shouldn't be a problem if I just plan to teleport in and out of Treoir before and after her visit."

Bernie shook his head. "You don't understand. She's coming to *stay* through New Year's."

"For two weeks? Are you freaking kidding me?"

"I know, right?" Bernie nodded with relief, as if that explained everything.

Tristan ground out, "*Why* is she coming here?"

"The guards said Macha wants a meeting with all the Alterants, but they heard that Evalle is spending the holidays here as a show of solidarity and support. Word is the Tribunal postponed their vote again on determining if we're a race until after the first of the year. Evalle wants to do her part and fly some of the security rounds to give all of us extra breaks."

Damn the Tribunal, run by deities who held the future of gryphons in their miserable hands.

Damn Evalle and her iron conscience, too.

Tristan's life would have been so much simpler if he'd just been born human, with no clue about all this preternatural crap.

Any other time, he'd appreciate Evalle's consideration, but right now her unyielding sense of honor was going to royally screw him, his foster sister Petrina, and Bernie. Tristan had teleported Petrina to Atlanta thirty-six hours ago. Once he brought her back to Treoir and recovered from teleporting, Bernie was to be Tristan's last trip. He'd hoped to spend some of the next two days in Atlanta while he waited to return Bernie.

Macha would call the gryphons to the castle the minute Evalle arrived in Treoir.

Bernie kept fidgeting. "Petrina has to be here."

"I know." Tristan and Bernie had to be on-site too.

If not, Macha would ... who knew what she'd do? But the fallout would be ugly and ruthless.

Tristan hated to do this to Bernie, but as their secret gryphon taxi to the human world, he had limitations.

"This changes things Bernie–"

Bernie broke in. "Don't even think about leaving me here. I have to go back to Atlanta."

"I can't physically teleport back and forth that quickly to take you, return Petrina here, then do another round trip to Atlanta and back with you." Tristan strained to take one person with him each way, since teleporting wasn't a natural gift, but something he'd gained from a dark source.

Bernie crossed his thin arms. "Take me when you go to get Petrina and leave me. You did that when you took Petrina and came back with Ixxter."

"That was an experiment, and the effort wiped me out."

"I understand and I'm sorry to ask that of you, but nothing has ever been this important to me. I've pulled double shifts just like everyone else. I want my time back home, just like the rest of them."

"I know you have, but–"

"No!" Bernie had never sounded so serious. "I haven't seen the woman I love since that dark witch captured me." His voice turned pitiful. "She's beautiful and I'm ... I'm not like you, Tristan. You walk through a room and panties fall off."

Tristan lifted his eyebrows at that.

Bernie dug in. "It's true and you know it. No woman looks at me like they want to jump *my* bones. I can't expect to ever find another woman even close to Claire."

What woman could be worth Bernie risking his life when he didn't make it back for Macha's meeting? Bernie's eyes took on the dreamy look of a man who had yet to learn the truth. A woman cared about only one thing–how much she could gain from a man.

Some would sell a guy out for a measly thousand dollars.

Bernie wouldn't stop once he got on something, dedicated as a dog with a meaty bone. "Women like Claire don't come along more than once. Ask Petrina. She'll tell you."

"Petrina? What are you saying, Bernie?" Honestly, the guy talked in circles half the time.

Bernie found his feet interesting all of a sudden. "I'm just saying that Claire is like Petrina. Special."

Tristan wasn't sure he liked this Claire being compared to Petrina. His sister could be a roaring pain some days, but she was solid and loyal.

He ignored his cramping muscles that wanted a long, hot shower and explained, "The minute Evalle leaves, I'll–"

That brought Bernie's head up. "No. Please, Tristan. I won't ask you to come back to the human realm for me, but I have to go there now. If I lose Claire, then surviving all this doesn't matter to me."

Shouting at Bernie that he needed to pull his head out of his ass would probably not help, so Tristan said, "If she truly loves you, she'll wait for you, right?" Not that he had any experience with love, but that seemed like a good benchmark.

"That's just it," Bernie explained. "Claire planned to stay in Atlanta until Christmas, then she was going home to be with her family in England. We talked about going together. I don't know where her family is in the UK, or how to find her if she leaves Atlanta. She has no idea I'm still alive. I had two weeks of heaven with her, and was on my way to meet her for dinner to propose. Then the witch showed up. She just wanted a monster to trade for Noirre majik, but she stole my only chance at happiness."

"You're not a monster," Tristan admonished lightly, although it was an apt description of all of the gryphons. But Bernie had enough self-esteem issues without adding another label.

"I know," Bernie mumbled then lifted his head. "Claire didn't see my green Alterant gaze until the night before I was grabbed. I never showed her my real monster side, but I'd love to show off my gryphon now. She'd keep my secret."

Tristan couldn't help the slither of suspicion that entered his thoughts. Five years ago, he'd lost his head over a woman. She'd seen his own glowing eyes the night before other Beladors captured him. Their warrior queen had sent Tristan to an invisible cage in a South American jungle.

And here I am, helping to protect that warrior queen.

Fate, meet irony.

In Bernie's shoes, Tristan would have questioned the timing of the witch finding him. "Are you sure you can trust this Claire?"

Meek little Bernie growled. "Don't you dare try to convince me that Claire had anything to do with a damn witch. She's very religious. She even offered to keep me safe until we could find a priest to help drive out the demon in me."

"You're not a demon either, dammit."

"I guess," Bernie mumbled.

"What do you mean, you guess? I know. I've fought demons. Just because we're Alterants who can shift into gryphons doesn't mean we're demonic in any way."

Bernie brightened at that. "I bet Claire would be impressed with my gryphon form, but I'd have to find a safe place to–"

Tristan lifted a finger and pointed it at Bernie. "Shift in the human realm, and you won't have to worry about Macha toasting you, not if the VIPER coalition gets their hands on you first. Humans can't know about any of us. Period. A VIPER patrol would pick you up and drop you at a Tribunal, and your pieces would end up scattered across the universe."

Bernie started to argue, but Tristan wasn't done. "And let's not forget that warlocks from the Medb coven are on the hunt for Alterants. If you'd wanted to face all that, you should have taken Evalle up on her offer to have Macha transport you back to the human world."

With the Medb and Beladors being dire enemies, the Medb were demanding half of the Alterants who had evolved into gryphons.

As though we're a bunch of livestock to be divided up.

Evalle had informed the gryphons of a Tribunal decision that forced Macha's hand. Any gryphon who wanted to leave Treoir would have to be teleported to the human world, courtesy of the goddess.

Out of the Belador frying pan into a Medb trap.

Bernie snorted with a shot of anger. "I didn't say I wanted to commit suicide. Evalle also said the minute Macha teleported *any* of us, Macha would have to inform the Tribunal of the gryphons who were available, so the Medb could *extend an offer* to join their coven. Medb warlocks would be all over my ass. I'd end up in their dungeon waiting to be used as a sacrifice, or worse."

"Exactly," Tristan snapped. When Evalle wasn't around, the responsibility of overseeing the group fell to Tristan. He was tired of playing counselor to this pack of gryphons. They had every right to complain, but he was sick of listening to it. "I haven't been risking all of our necks, slipping each of you into Atlanta one at a time, just to have you show off to some woman. If you make it back at some point, changing your form there *would* be suicidal."

The gryphons were all adults, and they knew the risks, but Bernie and Petrina might not be in danger right now if Tristan hadn't figured out that he could teleport between the Treoir realm and the human world.

And he couldn't snap his damn fingers and do it.

Twenty-first century Beladors lived among humans. They were part of VIPER, a force of powerful beings that protected humans. One sure way to get noticed, and not in a good way, would be to shift into gryphon form in the mortal world, where there was always a risk of being seen.

VIPER would release a hunt-to-kill order.

Carrying the blood of both camps put Alterant-gryphons in one hell of a tight spot.

If Tristan got caught leaving Treoir without permission, he didn't have enough fingers and toes to count all the ways he'd suffer and then die.

"I've flown extra hours for every gryphon here," Bernie went on. "I've never asked for anything except my fair share," he repeated.

True. Tristan let out a long sigh.

Why couldn't this be Ixxter's turn to go home? Ixxter was an asshole of the highest order, and Tristan wouldn't bat an eyelash at telling him no. Bernie went above and beyond for all the gryphons.

Every one of them had offered Tristan anything for a chance to go home this month for just two days.

He'd finally agreed, on one condition—everyone had to be in on this secret operation and cover for each other, plus fly double shifts to stretch the time they would not be expected to fly.

Everyone had agreed and carried their part.

Bernie *had* gone above and beyond. Tristan owed him an even bigger debt. Bernie had stepped in to protect Petrina during the recent Medb and Belador battle on this island.

Bernie deserved more than a damn teleporting trip.

But would he call in that marker right now?

No. *He's a better man than I am, because I would in his place if someone I loved waited for me.*

He hoped this woman was not making a chump of nice-guy Bernie.

For the millionth time, Tristan wished for a normal life, which was all Bernie really wanted, too. That had to be the reason Tristan said, "I'll take you with me, and I'll try to bring Petrina back then come for you. I have to return her first. She doesn't know about this, and you have the option of staying here safe."

Bernie's face went from hangdog to bursting with happiness. "Absolutely. I would never put my own safety ahead of Petrina's."

But you'd put a human woman ahead of your life. Tristan wanted to be happy for Bernie, but he couldn't trust a woman that easily. The wrong decision might cost Bernie his life.

The Alterants are adults. I can't make their decisions. Withholding his teleporting power from Bernie would be as wrong as it felt to take Bernie back with no guarantee Tristan could make that last trip.

Macha *could* torch all of the gryphons if she found out, but she wouldn't do that. She'd make an example of one, maybe two. She also saw them as valuable livestock, or she wouldn't waste her time on Tribunal meetings or argue so hard to keep them in her pantheon.

If Tristan believed the entire pack would be punished, he'd never have risked the first trip to the human world.

Once Tristan had Petrina back here safe, he'd make her swear to stay out of the way if there were repercussions, then Tristan would gut it out to return with Bernie.

"Thank you, Tristan. You'll be my best man."

Tristan didn't have the heart to point out that Macha was not going to allow any of them to live any kind of life with a human partner. But all Bernie wanted to do right now was go home and feel like a normal person for two days.

A troll friend of Tristan's had set up an apartment just for Petrina so she'd be safe in Atlanta. She stayed alone there, since all she wanted to do was watch her favorite movies, take long baths, and visit the Iron Casket nightclub, where strange was normal since a centaur owned it.

Every one of them had their own version of normal.

Bernie grinned from ear to ear. One big happy.

Disappointment stabbed Tristan at witnessing unbridled joy. He didn't begrudge Bernie some well-deserved happiness, but no one waited for Tristan.

He preferred it that way.

Keep telling yourself that.

He'd fallen for a woman once, only to have her stab him in the back. One day he would hunt down Elaine "Mac" Mackenzie, the one who'd sold him out for a thousand dollars.

That's all his freedom had been worth.

She'd done it the day after they'd spent the night together for the first time.

She would answer for every hellacious year he'd endured living alone and like an animal.

Tristan scrubbed his hands over his face, dismissing things that were out of his reach. For now. "Be ready to leave in an hour, Bernie."

"You can't go that soon. You normally need a full day after flying a double."

"Well, that's not going to happen, is it?"

"What are you thinking of doing?"

"I'm going to teleport every twelve hours to take you to Atlanta, bring Petrina back, return to Atlanta, and bring you back. The teleporting is going to suck, and you won't get two full days, but everyone gets their holiday visit and everyone comes home."

They would all return to Treoir *if* Tristan was correct about the minimum downtime required for him to teleport that many times in forty-eight hours.

This qualified him for the Stupid Idea of the Year award.

He hated holidays.

CHAPTER 2

"What the hell are you doing, Laney?"

Making a gamble with my entire future, but it's my gamble to take. Elaine Mackenzie shifted the phone between her chin and shoulder so she could balance her umbrella as she moved down the rain-wet street.

She hated to be called Laney, but her brother refused to call her Mac. "Last I checked, I'm working and paying my own bills, Brandon. I know that's a foreign idea for someone still living at home."

"I'm the person running our thirty-seven-room mansion, managing all the family financials, plus supporting Father's political career from down here now that he's in Washington. All that, plus keeping an eye on my errant sister, as if my other responsibilities aren't enough," he snarled. "Here's a novel idea for *you*—try pretending to be responsible. You're twenty-four-years old, for crying out loud. Show some appreciation to the family that raised you. Your room is still available if you can get your act together and stop chasing unicorns."

Unicorns. Her cheeks burned. He'd never let her forget what happened the week she turned nineteen.

Sarcasm was the least of Brandon's faults.

He snarled, "Hold on and don't you dare hang up."

A chill ran across her skin. She didn't live in the same house with him anymore. She was safe, to some degree.

Who are you kidding? She'd felt safe with a man one time in her life, and that night had turned out to be a mean joke on her.

A car raced by, throwing a knee-high wall of water against her jeans.

She had ten minutes to reach Inman Park by foot before the light rain gave way to the thunderstorm threatening downtown Atlanta. Why did it have to rain tonight when she'd planned to get Miss Wilma a Christmas tree? The eighty-eight-year-old woman had been a lifesaver since Mac's last apartment had burned. Mac had been walking Sampson, the elderly woman's Dachshund, during severe weather just to help her out. Then when Mac's apartment building went up in smoke, Miss Wilma invited Mac to share her Victorian cottage.

The sweet old lady had never asked anything of Mac since she'd moved in, but Mac had figured out that Miss Wilma longed for a tree to decorate.

Mac picked up her pace. First she had to change out of her best cable-knit sweater and spiked-heel boots. She needed flat-soled shoes and a poncho so she could carry a tree in this weather. She clutched an umbrella in one hand and her electronic tablet in the other while she jogged to beat the threatening downpour.

A lithe woman in neon yellow tights and matching top speed-walked by in the opposite direction, mocking Mac's definition of jogging.

She moved with such grace that rain seemed to dance off the bright yellow fabric.

Whatever. I'm not athletic.

Mac was physically strong and did mental gymnastics, so there. She slung a wet curl out of her eyes as Brandon clicked back on the line and started in on her again.

She talked over him. "I'm busy and I don't care what you think of my new job. Wait. Unless you think it's awesome ... in which case, I do care," she finished in the sweet tone she saved for children and idiots.

"Are you even listening to me, Laney?"

"It's been said that common sense is often an issue for geniuses, so let me analyze this for you, even though you did graduate from Harvard. Have you heard the distinctive click of disconnecting? Me neither. Therefore, it should be obvious I'm still listening, right?"

"You're not as funny as you think."

This man had destroyed her chance at a normal childhood and now he wanted to ruin the normal life she was trying to live. Brandon was a Mackenzie, and the men in her family put their public reputations above all else.

Never mar the perfect family image.

She'd been born a mistake and raised as a lie.

The minute she turned eighteen, she'd walked away with nothing and scratched out an existence. Brandon and his spin crew had done their usual job of turning her decision to "go it on her own" into more campaign fodder for her father, the senator. They played up how *he'd* raised a strong woman.

As if.

Wait, she did give them credit for hardening her heart. A shame it hadn't been enough to keep her from being devastated by a man with bright green—

"Laney!"

"What?"

"We allowed you to have your moment of independence. Father accepted that you needed some time to sow your oats."

She stopped and the rain tapped harder on her umbrella. If she could afford a new one, she'd sling her phone down on the ground so she could stomp his voice to death.

Don't destroy the phone your boss just gave you yesterday.

That calmed her down. "Are you on crack, Brandon? Sow my oats? I busted my butt every day between carrying a full load at college and working any minute I could. How dare you reduce it to nothing more than some act of defiance."

She'd hidden in corners her whole life, but her scholarship had given her the freedom she'd needed to leave home. Thanks to Jacob Kossman, who was also her new boss as of yesterday.

Every person had a breaking point.

Brandon didn't want to test Mac's again. Not now.

He'd terrorized her at sixteen, and she'd bloodied his nose when he'd tried to grope her. She'd threatened to tell their father. Brandon scoffed at her, convinced his father would believe him over her, which was true.

That night, she'd started sleeping with a knife under her pillow.

Senator Carson Mackenzie pretended he was a family man. Brandon pretended he loved his adopted sister. Another man had pretended to care about her, too, and that had been just as much a lie.

All men wore masks. She'd grown up in a family of pretenders. The scary part? She was better than all of them at hiding her feelings from the world.

Brandon only thought he knew the truth about her.

But right now she wanted to know what this call was really about, and his turning quiet was not a good sign.

Next would come his infuriatingly calm time-to-put-little-Laney-back-on-reality-highway voice.

Four, three, two, one …

Brandon pushed a loaded sigh through the connection. "Father called from China this morning. I promised him I would handle this issue before he returned, but I can't manage damage control without your cooperation."

Issue? Damage control?

This was her life, not a political campaign issue. Mac set her jaw. "There is no damage to control. I don't need your help with anything."

"Oh really? I've already had two calls from tabloids wanting the inside scoop on the poor little girl the Mackenzie dynasty raised and how we feel about her signing on with the eccentric Jacob Kossman."

The edge of her tattered self-respect frayed a bit and her glow of happiness dimmed a little. "It was a requirement as part of my scholarship deal."

"Which you should not have agreed to."

"That was *my* decision. You're just angry because you didn't know before now *and* because Kossman answers to no one, not even a Mackenzie."

Jacob Kossman funded laboratories all over the world and three specialized in rare genetics. One of those was right here in Atlanta. Years back, Mac had suspected her brother was behind the lack of scholarship offers from the ten schools she'd tried to get into, which was why she'd jumped at the scholarship to a university near Rome, Georgia. They were offering specific candidates a special chance to double major in an odd combination of genetics and mythological studies. Then she'd chosen the mythological studies program for her masters as the final part of that program.

Brandon and his father were not happy.

That alone made accepting the scholarship worth the snide remarks she'd suffered about studying fairy tales. The icing on the cake had been getting to delve deep into ancient accounts of the mystical, something she'd always found fascinating.

The scholarship had covered only part of her expenses. She'd racked up a few school loans on top of needing to actually eat regularly. So when Jacob Kossman offered her a chance to negate those school loans by accepting a position with his research empire for after graduation, she didn't hesitate. Yesterday though, she realized her job only waved a red flag in the face of her beast of a brother.

Because Kossman hadn't hired her for one of his labs where she could use her undergraduate degree in genetics.

He wanted her to use her mythological studies degree.

Didn't matter. She had the background and now she had a job. Kossman's deal would settle her scholarship contract if she stayed for two years, and the salary would allow her to buy a car and maybe find her own place to live. She would not sponge off Miss Wilma, and Mac wanted her own place, somewhere she'd feel good about inviting a man when she decided to date again.

The chances of dating happening any time soon were about as good as finding another guy with crazy green eyes.

Mac might not be entirely thrilled with her new job, but Brandon and *his* father no longer pulled the strings in her life.

She shoved warning into her voice to finish this conversation with Brandon. "Let me make myself clear. I have been paying my own way since I turned eighteen and I have asked for nothing." Except to be left alone.

"Must I remind you of your tenuous position that does not allow you to be cavalier when it comes to the media?"

Claws of dread climbed her spine at his not-so-subtle warning. "What are you saying?"

"That you aren't as smart as you think."

She knew just by his tone that he was not addressing her IQ. Had Brandon figured out that she'd been digging into the family background?

Mac would not allow Brandon to know how many nights she'd slept in terror, or how hard she'd worked at the self-defense classes she'd taken while in college. Still, the threat he'd thrown out so casually had the result he'd wanted. She stopped and caught her breath as a tingle of fear ran up her spine, then shook it off and forced confidence into her voice.

"I'm tired of you threatening me, Brandon. I've done my part as the Mackenzie charity case you and your father have turned me into. Poor little Elaine, adopted after she was found stuffed in a dumpster. I should be getting paid for all the good press you two have gotten from using me as a poster child for your supposed philanthropic endeavors. I owe you nothing. I'm out of your hair."

"As long as you walk around as a Mackenzie, you owe us everything. Don't ever think you don't."

Her fingers tightened on the umbrella to the point the cheap plastic handle squeaked in protest. If only she could tell the truth to the world, but the minute she did, her life would be forfeit. She'd end up in a dumpster for real.

Had Brandon discovered what she knew?

She'd once warned him that she'd left an incriminating letter with a person he would never find. Should anything happen to her that looked the least bit suspicious, it would be mailed to three major news outlets, as well as the senator's fiercest political enemies.

He'd laughed in her face and said, "Please give Father a reason to let me off the chain and send me after you."

She kept walking, ready to be warm and dry. "I know what you're capable of, Brandon, but if you think I'm crawling into a hole to keep you and your father happy, you have another think coming. No one cares that I'm working for Kossman unless *you* let them think it's an issue."

Brandon's words sounded as if he squeezed them from between clenched teeth. "You're drawing unnecessary media attention with this ghost-busting crap, plus there's a rumor that Kossman's going to support Dad's closest challenger for his seat.*"*

She muttered, "I should have known this was all about political games."

Now she understood why Brandon had his jockstrap twisted in a knot. She turned the media comment around on him. "Hey, you're the tabloid darling. Didn't I see a snippet on a rag cover about you in an intimate relationship with that *very* young movie star? What was she? Sixteen? The Mackenzie name survived that shit storm."

"No one bats an eye at sex these days," he said in dismissal. "How many times must I tell you that a Mackenzie doesn't use vulgar language? It shows a lack of breeding and education."

That was a load of crap. She'd heard both men drop F-bombs plenty of times, albeit behind closed doors.

She smiled, hoping it came through in her voice. "I doubt anyone will question my intelligence." She might not have inherited the Mackenzie good looks, but she tested off the charts when it came to IQ.

"Yes, yes, you do have a few brain cells. If you want to be taken seriously as a researcher, then don't accept a job hunting for goblins and fairies," Brandon said, changing his tactic.

Mac trudged on as the drizzle turned to showers. Why did home always feel twice as far away in dreary rain? Or maybe it was because of the conversation grinding on her nerves.

She dodged a deep rut in the broken sidewalk that had created a natural lake and argued, "Kossman's investment in researching rare DNA strains may one day offer insight into the genetic makeup of diseases such as Alzheimer's, leukemia–"

"Save that spiel for the media. You can paint this any way you want, but Kossman hired you for the Mackenzie name and your bizarre degrees. Everyone knows he wants to prove the supernatural exists, so don't try to sell him as some kind of trailblazer and that you're riding shotgun. Father has laboratory contacts all over the country. He'll find you a position paying whatever Kossman has offered. Maybe more."

Senator Mackenzie had gained a reputation of supporting medicine, but in truth that was about pandering to the elderly.

Mac would rather clean toilets than accept any position associated with the man who'd sired her. Yes, she knew Senator Mackenzie's dirty secret about her birth, but did Brandon? She didn't think so, or he'd find a way to drag her back to their mansion and put her under lock and key just to keep dear old Dad's secret safe.

She really shouldn't push Brandon when he was in his protect-the-Mackenzie-name mode, but it was hard to pass up a chance when she felt a moment of confidence. Still, if anything happened to Mac, who would watch out for Miss Wilma and her precious little Sampson? Not her two worthless children who lived on the West Coast, that's for sure.

Mac's phone buzzed with a text.

Kossman's ID came up on the display.

"I have to go, Brandon. I'm doing my best to stay out of your family's life. I suggest you all stay out of mine."

"Just remember that I tried to talk to you. You do what you have to and we'll do the same," he warned, then added, "and I know what you've been researching. Dump this job and come home, or you'll regret testing limits with me."

He hung up before she could ask what he'd uncovered.

She'd told no one about having her DNA tested. No, if Brandon knew the truth about her so-called adoption, he would have already silenced her. He knew *something*, but he was fishing.

The clouds unleashed buckets of rain, slapping the thin umbrella shielding her from a drenching. The oversized smart phone Kossman had given her was a nice perk, but her fingers weren't long enough to hold the phone and press the keys with one hand.

A white van pulled up on her side of the street and stopped near the curb. Water sloshed across the sidewalk. Rain pounded the ground in a roar. A thick-chested man who had a flat bulldog face and wore tactical gear exited from the passenger side.

She'd been introduced to Brewster Jennings yesterday, right after Mr. Kossman hired her. "What's going on, Brewster?"

"Mr. Kossman called and said he received word of a potential pre," Brewster explained. Kossman preferred the nickname "pre" to preternatural or supernatural. Pre would not create as much stir if overheard. Kossman's man said, "We were the closest team to you. He sent us to pick you up, Ms. Mackenzie. Said he'd text you."

"How did you fi–"

The phone. Clearly the nice perk had come with a GPS and location tracking activated, so her boss could always find her. Good to know.

She took a breath, not happy about her boss wanting her to drop what she was doing and go with Brewster. "In another two blocks I'll be home and I can–"

Brewster had reached for the door handle to the rear passenger area and paused to step over to her. "I realize you're new and may not understand how Kossman works. You got the first lead on a call, which has to mean he's either impressed with you or likes you or ... whatever, but the next tip goes to Seth Kako."

Mac and Seth had been placed in competition for the top position in Kossman's program. She would not lose that without a fight.

Brewster's rough voice rose to be heard over the increasing downpour. "Kossman's hell-bent to see this program succeed. I've been with him for almost two years and I respect the guy, even though this new job he's put me on is sometimes weird. You don't know him like I do, so here's a friendly tip. You have a small edge right now, but once you and Seth have delivered independent reports on specimens, Kossman will choose who to put in charge based on those reports. The person he designates as the head of this division in his program will have the power to hire ... and *fire*."

Kossman hadn't told her that.

Mac had met Seth Kako as she was leaving yesterday, and he didn't utter so much as a polite hello to her. His eyes sent the cold message that he intended to win that spot. He saw Mac as a threat, and rightly so. If he won the lead position, he'd fire her on the spot.

She needed this job and if she balked now, he could take it from her.

Would she ever get away from men and their threats?

Brewster stood there, water running off the night-vision headgear with its Terminator-looking monocular. "This is a Code Five to boot. We can't waste time."

"What's a Code Five?" She felt like an idiot, but she hadn't been clued in to anything that would involve men in tactical gear.

"A civilian has called in on the fifty-thousand-dollar bounty." At what had to be a confused look on her face, Brewster added, "Didn't Kossman mention field work?"

"Yes, but ... *bounties*? I thought ..." *What?* To be honest, she had heard "field work" and assumed she'd be going to research ancient writings. Besides, where would anyone come up with any being that fit Kossman's guidelines?

Could she actually do this job?

She had no choice and hadn't considered that Kossman would go to such lengths. She respected the man as a brilliant researcher, but she'd expected to test samples and write reports on *evidence* of strange creatures found in other countries.

Not someone here. Surely Brewster was not talking about someone ... human.

Brewster had been professional and patient with her, but his rapid-fire words indicated he was about to move on. "Kossman wants you on-site for consultation, in case we have any questions should there be a dispute later if this results in a capture."

Capture?

Capture *what*? She hated to admit Brandon was right about

anything, but he'd nailed the reality. This would trash her reputation in the research community.

If it got out.

It couldn't.

"Ms. Mackenzie?" Brewster said, and she knew it was his last attempt to sway her before he left her standing there.

She'd been upfront with Kossman about wanting to be a part of the new lab he was building for genomic medicine.

He agreed to consider her request if she proved valuable in his pursuit of uncovering supernatural abilities tied to blood.

This was an all or nothing deal with Kossman. She knew that when she originally took the scholarship, and yesterday when she signed on. And with Brandon breathing down her neck, she didn't have options. All or nothing. Against her better judgment, she was in. She had to be.

But, at the moment, she was most concerned about some unsuspecting person who was being set up or someone trying to scam Kossman.

"Just one more question, Brewster."

"That's more than I have time for."

"What exactly did someone call in about?"

"Something with glowing green eyes."

Blood rushed from her face, leaving her lightheaded. Not possible. Glowing green eyes. Again. "What else did—"

"I'm out of time, Ms. Mackenzie. You going or not?"

Oh, yes, she was going. She hurried toward the van, because she had to see this for herself and wanted to make sure nobody innocent was going to get hurt during this fiasco.

Green eyes.

Please, God, don't let there be any media on scene.

Kossman took his RUB–Research of Unusual Beings–operation *very* seriously. He'd fired someone over a media leak about hiring Mac, something that was to have been confidential.

He went to extreme measures to keep the media out of his business, and wanted no one privy to the details of his operation except a small circle, which now included her.

Okay, honesty time. Mac had always been curious about the unknown. That inquisitiveness, as much as her lack of options, had propelled her to accept the scholarship Jacob Kossman had offered where she could actually be taken seriously for her interest in the mystical. But she'd never expected this.

She settled on the back seat as Brewster shouted directions to the driver over the sound of the rain pounding the van roof. The driver looked just as broad shouldered and deadly as Brewster in matching tactical gear. The driver whipped the van back into traffic without a word or a glance at Mac.

She laid her collapsed umbrella in the floorboard and sniffed at the smell of worn leather and wet clothes.

Leaning forward, she put her hand on the back of Brewster's seat. "What are the chances of us getting lucky and this going down without attracting the press?"

Brewster grabbed the "holy shit" bar above the passenger seat as the van barreled around a hard corner. "Relatively good. Kossman's requirement for paying the bounty is that no media be present at the captures."

Mac breathed a little easier. "What type of ... being did the person say had these green eyes?" Maybe it was some four-legged animal.

Brewster looked over his shoulder. The grim cut of his mouth and brutal gaze promised anything deadly would have an equal match. "All I know is we're after something that looks human but he has glowing eyes."

He? No, no, no. This couldn't be happening.

She stared openmouthed as Brewster turned back around to take a call. She shivered, as if ants with tiny claws ran along her arms and neck.

This could not be happening.

Brandon had to be behind the bogus bounty report. There *would* be media present, because Brandon wasn't after the bounty money.

That bastard had called her for one reason. So that once everything went sideways and the media nightmare started, he could tell his father that he'd warned her. Senator Mackenzie would lose his shit over this and Brandon would call her, offering to make it all go away if she returned to the Mackenzie prison.

But she couldn't stop the van from barreling toward disaster. Not with a human possibly at risk. It couldn't be *him,* but it was someone else at risk of being harmed.

If Mac bailed out now before she knew for sure what waited at the end of this trip, her deal with Kossman would vanish.

She'd be lucky to find work anywhere. Brandon had been thorough in limiting her choices years ago. She had no doubt he'd already squashed her chances of a job of consequence—without accepting his offer—even at an environmental lab, where she'd be shoved in a corner testing dirt samples and never seen or heard from again.

Maybe she could change her name and disappear.

If so, her next job would require her to ask, "Do you want fries with that?"

If this bounty call turned out to be a trap Brandon had set, complete with media ready to expose this "capture," Kossman would blame her for the leak.

Glowing green eyes.

Not possible.

CHAPTER 3

"The point was to stay out of sight once we reached Atlanta." Tristan wiped water off his face, shook out the baseball cap, and shoved it on his head again. He trudged through water puddles, pissed at everything, but mostly at the chump striding next to him.

Bernie murmured, "I know."

Tristan ground his teeth. "Let me get this straight. The person now living in your girlfriend's old apartment was nice enough to let us use the phone, but this woman you want to marry can't drive over and pick us up?"

Bernie raised his shoulders then hunched them in again. "Claire said she had some drops put in her eyes today and can't drive in the rain."

Bullshit. Tristan kept that thought to himself.

He had a bad feeling about this woman Bernie wanted to stick a diamond ring on. Bernie had dated her for all of two weeks. Did he really think that was enough time to see someone's true colors?

Who am I to criticize? I met a woman and fell for her in ten days.

How'd that work out?

Not very well. *Chump.*

Bernie stumbled and had to do an awkward dance to keep upright. He rubbed at his eyes. "I can't see through these stupid contacts at night."

"Then put on the damn sunglasses, because I don't care," Tristan said, indicating the pair hooked on the front of Bernie's shirt. "No one can know that either of us is here. The minute a human sees glowing green eyes, they'll go apeshit and call out the National Guard, which I'm pretty sure is full of Belador warriors."

With the contacts in, no humans would recognize them ... unless they used kinetics or other powers to stop a preternatural predator.

Beladors were another story.

"I know, I know," Bernie grumbled, stuck on two words like a corrupted audio. Rain drizzled down the side of his neck. "What are you going to do once we get to Claire's?"

First, I'm waiting around to make sure she doesn't have some witch waiting for you. Tristan answered, "I have a place to hole up while I wait."

He'd have to walk there, though. A few months ago, he'd downed a witch highball infused with ancient Kujoo warrior blood, and teleporting had been one of the side benefits. But using that gift drained his energy, especially when traveling from one realm to another like he'd just done with Bernie.

Otherwise his ass wouldn't be stuck walking in the damn rain. They could run fast as hell due to their Belador blood, but Tristan was saving every ounce of energy to take Petrina home and make one more round trip for Bernie before Macha's meeting.

Evalle couldn't be happy about leaving Storm and her pet gargoyle at home, but she was too damned honorable for her own good sometimes. She would never ask Macha to put off a meeting that was probably all bullshit.

Tristan had tried to tell Evalle not to trust Macha or VIPER. Evalle kept trying to convince Tristan that the Alterant-gryphons would one day be a free race.

But that hadn't happened.

She'd also warned him not to screw up while he was on Treoir, since Macha was the only goddess in their corner.

That was yet another reason Tristan had to return with Bernie and Petrina before Evalle arrived on Treoir. She had no idea that Tristan had tested his teleporting ability and found out he could travel between realms.

But he couldn't risk trying to travel with Bernie and Petrina at the same time without enough power or he might kill all of them.

Bernie rubbed at his eyes. "These things interfere with my kinetics, too."

"What makes you say that?"

Bernie lifted both hands. "Watch." For about thirty seconds, the rain shed away from them as though they were under a small dome, but then it started leaking through.

That's not good. Tristan rubbed his forehead, which now

throbbed from lack of sleep.

Bernie looked over. "Did you hear me?"

"I heard the word *watch*."

"After that, I spoke to you telepathically."

"Shit." The damn contacts were screwing up kinetics *and* communication. They irritated Tristan's eyes, too, but he hadn't needed to talk to anyone telepathically while wearing them. He'd had the contacts made to insure each person he delivered to this world would be as safe as possible while here. His troll buddy, Otto, had come through with the majik enhanced contacts, but they lasted only forty-eight hours.

Bernie kept speeding up. Then he'd pause when he realized what he was doing and slow back down to human pace. "I can't wait to see Claire."

Tristan finally said what was eating at him. "It still bothers me about the timing of the witch capturing you the day after you showed Claire your eyes."

Bernie turned a furious gaze on Tristan. "Stop trying to make me doubt her."

Tristan had a sick feeling this would not play out the way Bernie expected. He'd heard Claire's voice when Bernie called her. She hadn't sounded like a woman relieved to hear from her lost love.

Hell, Tristan had far more experience with women than Bernie, but he'd allowed a woman to lead him right into a trap.

Mac had smiled at him.

He'd been stupid to be hooked by a smile, but Tristan had been on the receiving end of those so rarely that one look at Mac's sweet lips had made his brain shut down.

He'd wanted her, and nothing could stop him when she invited him into her bedroom. He'd known better.

Humans were a risk.

They panicked at anything unexpected.

Ten days after meeting accidentally in Piedmont Park and returning every evening to find her waiting on him, he'd wanted her but he'd had no plan to pursue her.

Not until a guy hiding a blade fell into step behind her as she headed home one night.

Tristan had made a habit of following her discretely to know she made it home safely, then going his own way, but that night changed everything. He caught up with Mac and her shadow just as the guy poked his knife tip into Mac's back.

She'd made a noise of fear, and Tristan had to remind himself to not kill the human. Not unless he harmed Mac. Tristan wrapped his arm around the neck of her attacker, disarmed him, and sent him flying into a tree.

That had rung the bastard's bell.

While Tristan convinced Mac to not call the police department, which was full of Beladors working covertly, the thug vanished into the dark.

Mac looked up at Tristan as if he'd saved her from a demon, then she took his hand and led him into her apartment. He'd told her he couldn't take his glasses off and she hadn't cared.

Yeah, the small head had made that decision.

He'd had rare opportunities to be with a woman, and never stayed, but for some reason he'd slept like the dead. When he opened his eyes at daylight, she had his sunglasses in her hand. With one look, she'd scrambled off the bed and backed away.

He explained that he had a rare case of *tapetum lucidum* syndrome, which made his eyes glow like cat or deer eyes at night.

Mac had acted as if she accepted his story, but he'd been a fool.

A team of Beladors had found him the next day.

Still, just because the woman Tristan had trusted turned out to be a liar didn't make Bernie's girlfriend one. Bernie deserved a chance to have someone special.

Tristan would never make that mistake again.

Rain slowed to a steady shower as Tristan led Bernie through the dark residential streets of Avondale Estates, to a small house with a wide porch.

"This is it!" Bernie bounced and pointed.

Tristan cautioned, "Remember what I told you. If anything happens–"

"I know. I know. Find your sister in Decatur and go to the meeting point with her tomorrow to find out what you want to do. Don't let anyone follow me to Petrina's place, and don't shift from my human form. I got it, *Mom*."

"How did you survive so long around Ixxter with that smart mouth of yours?"

Bernie grinned. "I'm a charmer."

"You're not charming me right now."

"You're not my type."

"Agreed." Tristan stopped in the front yard as Bernie walked up concrete steps to a small stone-and-brick house. His fist drummed the wooden door.

A porch light glared on.

Shouldn't that have been on already?

Tristan would normally cover his eyes, but the dark brown contacts dulled the glare.

If he had telepathy right now, he could talk to Bernie without anyone hearing. Everything came with a price.

Bernie knocked on the door again with anxious beats. "I'm here, Claire. It's me. Open up."

A muffled female voice said, "Hold on, Bernie."

Tristan tensed.

He hated to be right, but why wasn't she rushing out to meet Bernie? Had she changed her mind about their relationship? Why tell Bernie where she lived if she didn't want to see him again?

Shadows from sprawling oak trees blocked much of the streetlight, and the damn contacts were limiting what he could see. His night vision was excellent, though it was nothing like Evalle's ability to see in the dark. Her eyes were ultra-sensitive to light and the sun would cook her body to a crisp.

Yeah. He'd keep his vision. Tristan cut his gaze to the side, tracking a figure that slid from a white van parked a block away. Shadows the size of human bodies moved through the dark and pulled up behind a thick oak tree.

Tristan didn't detect any power signature.

A human ambush?

Bernie's voice crashed from happy to desperate. "Claire?"

Shit. Tristan whispered, "Bernie! Get down here."

But Bernie was as focused on Claire as a male dog catching the scent of a bitch in heat.

Appropriate analogy.

Tristan moved slowly toward the porch to keep from giving away that he'd recognized the threat moving in. Who had Claire called in and why? How would she know preternaturals to contact?

Had she been the one to hand Bernie to the witch after all?

There was no way Tristan could teleport even one of them out of here right now, but maybe he–

"Don't move." That order boomed from a man whose upper body would qualify him to arm wrestle the Hulk in his spare time. He wasn't APD or SWAT, but he was dressed for combat. The weapon he pointed could be the bastard child of an H&K rifle and a stormtrooper's laser blaster.

Commando guy said, "We know what you are. Come with us quietly and we won't hurt you."

Human? Tristan still hadn't picked up on any odd energy. He arched an eyebrow at that order and crossed his arms. "Here's a better idea. Leave us alone and *I* won't hurt *you*."

Bernie must have finally figured out that he'd been screwed without a kiss. He trudged down the steps to join Tristan and muttered, "She doesn't love me."

Tristan ignored him and kept his gaze on the threat. "Pay attention."

Bernie's head snapped up and he started trembling.

Another guy dressed identically in black cargo pants, a tactical vest, and matching weapon stepped from behind a thick oak tree. He yelled, "Put your hands up now!"

Shit. Tristan had no idea if those weapons worked on nonhumans, but a blast exploding the head worked on pretty much everyone.

Tristan had no doubt Bernie's girlfriend—*ex*-girlfriend—had called in this goon squad. But what would humans be after?

More importantly, who was paying for this?

A third person climbed out of the van and headed their way. This one wore a hooded, dark-gray raincoat that looked too big for the short stature. A voice called out, "Wait, Brewster."

A female?

Brewster must be the guy in charge. He answered, "I told you to stay back until I have them contained."

This looked worse every second.

The woman argued, "You can't do this or–"

Brewster lifted his hand. "I'm not doing anything yet. If everyone stays calm, no one gets hurt."

Tristan couldn't make the same promise. If he and Bernie were caught outside of Treoir, Petrina would be left vulnerable to VIPER and the Beladors. If Macha didn't have Bernie or Tristan in hand to make an example of, she would use Petrina the minute she found her. Tristan would suffer Macha's anger, but he would not let the goddess take her wrath out on Petrina, or even Bernie.

He raised his hands slowly, in the universal sign of surrender, and whispered out the side of his mouth to Bernie, "Get ready to run back the way we came the minute I say go. Don't stop until you find Petrina."

Bernie lifted his shaking hands and whispered back, "You're not going with me?"

The two men took a step into the open then another toward Tristan and Bernie, weapons pointed.

Tristan told Bernie, "No. Use your preternatural speed. Don't allow anyone to follow you to her apartment."

Bernie whined, "I don't want to leave you."

"If you don't do what I say, you'll get me killed first, then you and Petrina," Tristan said, tapping Bernie's protective nature toward Petrina. His words were little more than a bluff. He *should* be able to defend himself against a trio of humans, but those weapons were odd. Anyone who intentionally hunted a preternatural would come loaded to take down the Kracken.

The woman in the oversized raincoat squeezed closer to Brewster and whispered, "This is a mistake. I don't see glowing eyes. Mr. ... our boss would not sanction this."

Brewster half turned to answer her. "Doesn't matter. He pays me to deliver anything and anyone he sends me after. I'm taking this one in. The boss can decide what happens at that point."

"But this doesn't look right," the woman said. "He won't be happy about you harassing a *human*."

Brewster's attention wavered only a second.

That was enough.

Tristan took advantage of the discord and ordered Bernie, "Run. *Now!*"

Bernie lit out of there faster than a cat with its tail on fire. With Belador speed, he'd turned into a blur.

Brewster jerked up his weapon.

Tristan pushed the palms of his hands forward and hoped like hell *his* kinetic wall would hold.

Brewster and his sidekick activated their laser weapons.

The woman jumped up and shouted, "*No!*"

Her hood fell back, revealing her face.

Tristan's jaw fell open. *No fucking way.* His kinetic shield shattered beneath heavy laser fire.

Power struck him in the chest.

It lifted him a foot off the ground. He bellowed in pain and arched, muscles tight and fists shaking. Taking a lightning bolt through his chest couldn't hurt this much. Energy blazed across his skin.

The last thing he saw was Elaine freakin' Mackenzie's terror as the world turned gray.

Bernie had gotten away.

Tristan's feet hit the ground. He fell to his knees with only one wish.

Please let me live long enough to strangle Mac for doing this to me again.

CHAPTER 4

Tristan was back.

Mac knelt in the back of the van next to his still body. She'd covered him with her raincoat, but he was showing no sign of life. She yelled at the two men in the front of the van, "How could you shoot him? He was unarmed."

"I didn't shoot him. These are Nyght stun guns."

"Night? Guns?"

He spelled it out. As if that helped.

She had no idea who Nyght was, or what kind of gun Brewster carried, but the strike had taken Tristan off his feet and blue energy had covered his body.

How could any human survive that kind of power?

Maybe he's not human after all.

She rolled her eyes and forced that thought back into the corner of her mind where curiosity bubbled nonstop, and where she'd shoved that thought so long ago when she'd first been taken in by his little joke. Tristan clearly did not have glowing green eyes now, which confirmed that "bad joke" was the right thing to call what he'd done. In fact, his eyes had looked brown when the light hit his face. The blast had been similar to a lightning bolt, but people survived lightning strikes and those had to be more powerful, right?

Brewster called back, "He's alive, right? Mr. Kossman will be pissed at the Nyght weapons group if their stun gun killed a specimen."

She warned Brewster, "You'd better hope he doesn't die, or you'll have worse to face than Kossman." She'd turn that damn gun on the lot of them and see how they liked it.

Sure, she was still angry with Tristan, but she had not signed on to attack humans, or nonhumans, with weapons of any kind.

Kossman had some explaining to do.

This couldn't be what he had in mind for her or the program.

He'd never seemed like the kind of man who would endorse attacking a defenseless human. Had Brewster been so determined to please Kossman that he'd made this decision on his own? She didn't know, but there would be no repeat of this event, not with her involved.

Her hands were finally warm enough to feel for a pulse in Tristan's cold wrist.

How could he be back? Okay, Atlanta was a big city. Maybe he'd never really left at all. Just walked away from her. But why had he been targeted when he clearly did not have glowing eyes?

She'd wanted to choke him back then for the ugly prank—and for what he'd done to her heart.

Now she feared he might be dying. Or was he already dead? She kept feeling for a pulse.

Brewster yelled at the driver, *"Look out!"*

Something slammed the side of the van. They skidded and spun, then were hit again. The van lifted up on one side, rolling over.

Mac screamed and went airborne.

Hands snatched her out of the air as the van banged over on its side, then rolled onto the roof, then back onto its other side. She rolled over and over, bouncing against walls, but she wasn't hitting hard or getting banged up much, which made no sense.

Everything happened so fast, then suddenly nothing.

The van had stopped upright, but tilted at an angle. The motor still ran. Mac's heart fought inside her chest. She sucked air in gulps. She tried to push up, but she was pinned down to ... Tristan's body.

His arms were banded around her. That's what had kept her from being bashed. But what about him? First stunned with those blasters and now bounced in a rolling van. How was he even conscious?

She whispered, "Tristan?"

"Shh. Be quiet. Don't let them know you're awake." He'd given that order in a taut voice.

Before she could ask what he was talking about, his arms flopped loose just before the rear door opened and a harsh voice demanded, "What the hell? Which one of those two is the target?"

"Don't know. Let's take both and sort it out later. We gotta go."

Tristan's lips moved against Mac's skin when he softly said, "Act limp and unconscious."

Her heart was beating too fast for her to pretend to be unconscious. Who had hit their van and what did they want?

She lifted her lashes enough to see that one man was directing another man who backed a panel truck.

She whispered, "Who are they?"

Tristan sighed. "I don't know. Don't ask."

She hissed, "Why?"

"Because I said so, dammit." He sounded pissed, but he had reason to be after this insane capture.

She narrowed her eyes at the familiar comment. Growing up around male arrogance had immunized her. Ordering her around hadn't worked on her in the past, and it wouldn't now either.

But when the two men came back to pull her out of the van, some innate sense told her to do as Tristan said. He sounded as if this was not unusual for him, but Mac had zero experience with getting kidnapped. She stayed quiet and limp while someone carried her to the panel truck, where he tossed her in.

Literally tossed her.

She clamped her jaws to keep from groaning when she landed hard on her shoulder and it popped. Hot pain blinded her.

Don't say a word. She clenched her teeth and tried not to move. Tears stung the corners of her eyes. If she'd ended up facing the rear of the truck, her captors would have known she was conscious by the way she bit down on her lip. She took shallow breaths, trying to hold on to her composure.

A body dropped behind her and the doors slammed shut on the back of the box truck. The sound of a heavy lock being snapped followed. No chance of getting out of here.

As soon as the truck took off, excruciating pain shot through her shoulder and upper arm. Mac couldn't stifle a cry at the movement and rolled onto her back, gasping to keep from throwing up.

Tristan's inert form came to life beside her. "What's wrong?"

#

Stupid contacts. Tristan couldn't see Mac's body clearly in the back of this pitch-dark, enclosed truck bed. Without the contacts, he'd be able to see in here, but removing them would be a mistake even though Mac had seen his eyes in the past. Once the contacts came out, they couldn't be used again. He didn't want to confirm he was nonhuman to anyone else until he had no choice.

The less his captors knew, the better.

Finally, he had the woman who'd stolen his freedom. He'd waited five years to pay her back, and now he had her alone and at his disposal.

So what are you going to do, chump?

You'd think he'd have spent every minute of those five years planning her death, or at least some degree of torture.

But no. A sigh broke loose from him. Good thing no one could hear his thoughts, or his dickhead reputation would take a hit.

The diesel engine and road noise drowned out most sounds, but he was sure he'd heard Mac moan.

Was she pretending so he wouldn't kill her, or had that been a true sound of pain?

He asked, "Are you hurt? What's wrong?"

"Landed hard. Think they dislocated my shoulder."

Yep, that hurt. He'd done that to his own shoulder once, and if not for his beast power, he wouldn't have been able to fix it. Even then, he'd yelled at the top of his lungs, pissed and in agony.

Why wasn't she screaming her head off?

Because I told her to be quiet. If he were as dedicated to payback as he'd thought, his gut wouldn't be churning at the idea of her in the kind of pain he'd suffered.

Now he wished he'd fought the two trolls that captured them, but with his power at a trickle, he might have gotten Mac killed even if *he* had survived.

He could still regenerate from death one more time. Maybe. He wasn't sure that worked unless he was in gryphon form. Talk about a screwed-up heritage.

And why would it matter if Mac died, chump?

What the ever-loving goddess had brought on all the fucking yammering going on in his head? Until he made up his mind what to do with Mac, no one killed her but him.

That should shut up his rogue conscience.

She sucked in a harsh breath and his conscience thumped him again.

Tristan dug into his pocket for the extra key to Petrina's building. It had a tiny LED light the size of a quarter on it. When he flashed it on, Mac turned her head away, but not before he saw the tear tracks running down her face.

He said, "Hold this for me so I can take a look."

"Why?"

Obstinate woman. "I can fix your shoulder, but I need to be able to see."

"Do you have a medical background?" she asked in a snappy voice.

Pain pissed him off, too, but he wasn't looking for any sort of connection between them, so he answered in a surly voice. "Sort of."

She turned back to him. "Is your medical degree *sort of* like having glowing eyes?"

Does she think these are my normal eyes? No, she had to be jerking his chain. They'd have the conversation about his eyes and this unfinished crap later, once he fixed her shoulder and put her back on even ground with him.

That way, she couldn't blame him for taking advantage of her weakened situation. "I didn't say I had a medical degree, but I can fix your arm."

"Don't touch me–" The truck bounced over a bump. She clenched her teeth and whined in pain.

What reason did *she* have to sound angry? He hadn't captured her and put her ass in this mess.

He wouldn't waste the time finding out right now when he had no idea how long this ride would be. "I *can* put the bone back into the socket, but you have to help by relaxing. Yes or no? Make up your mind."

A tear slid down the side of her nose.

He'd never seen her cry. He didn't like watching the tears snake down her face now.

Tristan growled, "Just hold the damn light, would you?"

She must be ready to rip her arm off for relief. Without looking at him, she lifted her good arm and opened trembling fingers. Tristan placed the LED between her index finger and thumb, closing them carefully.

He told her, "Point the light down so you don't blind me."

When she did, he finally got a look at her shoulder. This was going to hurt like a son of a bitch.

He'd barely touched her arm and she hissed, *"Don't!"*

"The longer you wait, the harder this will be, Mac."

She muttered something about that being easy for him to say. That mouth hadn't changed a bit in five years. Constantly asking questions or debating whatever anyone said.

But now that he could see more of her, it was obvious she'd grown up since the last time they were together. The soft curves were still there, but she had a sharpness about her that didn't fit the sweet young woman he'd met in Piedmont Park so long ago.

The same woman who sent you to South America in chains the first time, and played a role in your capture tonight.

True, and he wanted to give her a piece of his mind, but not while she ground her teeth in pain. Even he wasn't that much of an asshole. He'd get his chance to ask her why she'd turned him over to the Beladors so long ago.

Did she even know who the Beladors were?

She pretty much had to for them to come after Tristan when he was captured. Right? But they were hypervigilant about secrecy, so how could she have known of them? He'd wanted that answer for a long time.

Mac turned to face him, but kept the light pointed down, which left his face in shadows. "What makes you think you can do anything with my shoulder?"

Surviving all those years in a dangerous jungle made him a fucking expert. "If you'll stop the twenty questions and work with me, this will go faster."

"Not until you explain how you're going to–"

Tristan sighed, gently grasped her injured arm and she shut up with a hiss. In that moment, he couldn't deny it. He hated seeing the woman he'd once cared for hurt.

Exhaustion had to be messing with him, but as much as he wanted to lash out at her, he gentled his voice. "Just relax."

If he'd been a normal human, he'd have to put his foot against her torso to do this, but even at low energy he still had supernatural strength. He only had to put one hand under her arm to push against her body for leverage.

Bad idea. His fingers were inches from her breast. What kind of horn-dog thought about a woman that way when he was supposed to be helping her? *Me, evidently.*

He closed his mind to everything except gently pulling on her arm as she panted and made noises that were gutting him. Could he ease her pain the way he'd once used his energy to help heal a nonhuman?

Tristan called up his beast and fed healing energy down his arm to his hand that touched her body.

Sweat ran into his eyes, in spite of the cold air.

The shoulder popped back into the socket.

Relief flooded him. He let out a breath, not questioning why her being hurt stressed him so much.

When he looked down, he found Mac sniffling, but she hadn't made a sound the men in the cab might have heard over the road noise and rumble of the diesel engine. Damn, but he admired her grit. "Are you okay, Mac?"

"Yes... I'm surprised the pain is easing, but I've never had a shoulder go out like that so I guess ... that's normal, huh?" she answered with a swipe of confusion in her voice. "I feel a weird ... sizzling where you're touching me."

"Just the feeling coming back to some of the nerve endings," he said, pretty sure that was a lie. He moved his hand quickly, thankful his beast energy actually did something for her.

But she didn't think he had glowing eyes.

That made no sense. She *knew* he had glowing eyes. She'd seen them.

She acted as if she didn't know he was a nonhuman.

A thought hit Tristan square in the chest. *Someone* had turned him in, just like Claire had done to Bernie tonight. What if that someone was not Mac? Tristan dug through old memories, trying to sort through what had happened and who owed him for lost time. Could she have said something back then to a human who knew of the Beladors?

Or more likely, said something about glowing eyes to a Belador she *thought* was a human?

If so, that would mean he'd spent five years hating her for no reason.

Mac wasn't the only one confused.

What had really happened back then? He started to ask, and got sidetracked when her teeth chattered.

Crap. She had to be freezing between the cold air, the metal truck bed, and the shock of being hurt.

Touch her again or not?

Yes, he wanted to, but what man wouldn't want to hold this woman in his arms?

Even after all the shit he'd been through with getting captured, and all the time he'd spent in the bowels of jungle hell, his stupid heart thumped hard when he looked at her. In his mind, he still saw the sweet young woman who'd waited for him each day after they'd met.

Waited just to talk.

That had been the closest he'd ever come to normal in his life.

His head kept reminding him that she *could* have been behind his capture, and he had no business touching her any more than necessary.

His heart didn't have a lick of sense, and kept pounding loud enough to drum out the noises in his mind.

When she shivered hard, Tristan reached down and lifted her into his arms.

Mac tensed.

He stopped moving. "What?"

"Nothing ..." She relaxed and let out a sound that was a mix of weariness and acceptance. "Okay, I can admit my arm is feeling better every second. Thank you. I'm amazed at what you did. Where did you learn how to do that?" She kept the LED on, but with that arm hanging at her side, she had the light pointed down, giving off a soft, ambient glow.

And we're back to twenty questions.

He settled her in his arms and turned to lean his back against the metal wall. "I spent a lot of time alone in South America where I had to take care of my own injuries."

"So that's where you went," she murmured. "What were you doing there?" She stared up at him with eyes lacking the devious quality he'd expected. She looked completely innocent of any crime.

Doubt scampered through his chest. Was this an act or real?

He wanted answers, too, and tossed back, "That's where I was sent after you alerted someone to my existence."

"What are you talking about?"

He studied her face. "I was grabbed the day after you saw my green eyes. Who'd you tell about me?"

"I asked my professor and some students about your condition, which clearly was not a condition, but a lie. I could have accepted that you played a practical joke on me, but not the way you left, and now this ... *story*."

He thought back over everything that had happened. "Damn."

"What?"

"I bet one of your professors was a Belador."

"A bella-what?"

"Never mind. So you had nothing to do with me being captured?"

"You were *captured*?" The astonishment in her voice sounded sincere. She breathed deeply, and on the exhale said, "If that's true, I don't feel so bad about you disappearing on me. I've been pissed at you for five years. Why would you think I'd be behind someone capturing you and keeping you in South America, Tristan?"

He stared at her, trying to accept what she was saying, but still not sure what to believe. "If you really weren't behind that, what were you doing tonight, with men carrying those kinds of weapons?"

"I don't know anything about the weapons except that they're Nyght stun guns."

"Stun guns? They hit me with enough charge to take down a pack of stampeding elephants, but that makes sense if it's a Nyght weapon. I've heard about those."

"Oh, please." She cocked her chin at him with a wry grin. "Exaggerate much? If the stun had been that powerful, you'd be dead. It doesn't excuse them for mistreating you, but that's a bit much. And who or what is Nyght?"

Did that mean she didn't realize that he was an Alterant? "It's a weapon designed for specific use," he hedged. "Who were those men and what were you after?"

"*I* wasn't after anything," she said indignantly. "I was only there as a consultant."

"What kind of consultant?"

She became very still. "You'll laugh."

"No I won't." Not much.

"I just signed on with Jacob Kossman."

"That name means nothing to me," he lied. He'd heard rumors about Kossman's supernatural encounter years ago, but wanted to see what Mac would say.

She took his measure with her next look. "Have you been living under a rock? Kossman's in the news every other week."

"I told you I was out of the country."

"Oh, right. He's a mega billionaire who is mostly known for his international enterprise in medical-research-based, unusual healing methods and medicines, and ... uh, other types of research. I went to a university he built."

"And you're a consultant for him? Doing what?"

She huffed with a defeated sigh. "Might as well tell you. Kossman is considered an eccentric, and I got my degree from the Titan University of Georgia. It's north of here, in Rome. Years ago, Kossman claimed to have had an experience with a supernatural being. He's obsessed with investigating the unusual."

"A ghost hunter?"

"No. I'm tired of everyone calling this ghostbusting," she groused. "Kossman thinks supernaturals walk the earth, and he's determined to prove it. I graduated at the top of my class and he noticed. I have a chance at a really good position with him later, and I'll dress up as a wookie if that's what it takes to win it, so when his men picked me up to join them, I didn't really have a choice."

Warning. Danger zone. Tristan scratched his chin. "So what did you and your two gunmen *think* you were going to find tonight?"

She whipped an angry gaze at him. "They were not *my* gunmen. They said Kossman wanted me on-site to consult on a potential target."

"Which was?"

She rubbed her hands over her eyes. "Where is a bottomless sinkhole when I need one?"

Tristan fought a smile at the reminder of the woman he'd met years back, who would always say whatever was on her mind.

She dropped her hands and stared at the other side of the truck body. "Apparently they had a report from a woman who claimed that she'd met a guy earlier this year. He supposedly had green eyes that glowed and claimed he could change his body into a beast. She said he'd disappeared for a few months and had just turned up again. He called her tonight and said a witch had captured him, but he was now free. She called in on Kossman's tip line for a bounty fee, and said she'd told the green-eyed guy to come to her new apartment."

That bitch, Claire. Tristan swallowed the "I told you so" hanging on the tip of his tongue. Bad as this was, poor Bernie had gotten his heart ripped out.

Tristan asked, "So you didn't know I was going to be there?"

She twisted around, a frown marring her face. "Why would I? And what were you doing there?" Then it hit her. "I'm an idiot. I thought my br—" She swallowed that word and continued. "I thought someone was setting up me and my boss to be embarrassed by the media with the whole glowing eyes crap. Now I get it. This was a scam to get the money, wasn't it?"

"I don't know. How much money?"

"Fifty thousand. Are you in cahoots with that woman who called?"

"No. The guy she was talking about is a friend of mine. I was just in the wrong place at the wrong time."

Mac didn't look like she believed him, but he wouldn't believe it either if the tables were turned. Shit. Did VIPER know someone was after Alterants and other nonhumans?

Would they care? Yes ... if humans got involved, which had happened tonight. Tristan had to leave here with information so he'd know how to protect his pack of Alterant-gryphons. But who would he tell?

No one could find out he'd left Treoir.

Much as he wanted to prevent Mac from learning the truth, his first priority was her safety. He had to let her know what they were up against for any chance of getting her out of here.

Not that he had any intention of playing white knight. With his black soul, he was far from a savior, but he couldn't let her continue naively thinking this was a basic kidnapping.

One thought kept poking at him.

Mac had not turned him in the first time.

The Beladors who took him captive had said something about a woman getting her Alterant fee. He'd put two and two together, and come up with Mac as the one at fault.

The truck slowed, as if it had reached a destination.

No time to waste. He turned to Mac. "Listen to me and do what I say if you want to get out of this alive."

"We'll be rescued as soon as they send a ransom demand to Kossman. I just need you to pretend to be a supernatural being until we get to Kossman, then I'll explain and he'll understand the lie, considering the circumstances. Can you do that?"

What? Tristan paused at the sound of voices yelling outside the truck, but couldn't make out the words. The truck pulled forward slowly. "They may or may not be asking for money."

She frowned. "Why wouldn't they?"

"Because they're not human. The two guys who tossed us in here are trolls. They want me because I'm what's called an Alterant, and even if they are after a bounty fee, it may have nothing to do with Kossman."

Mac's face swirled with confusion then her eyes narrowed. "Really? What is it with you wanting to be some comic book character? I actually believed you the first time and where did that get me? It wasn't bad enough you broke my–" She clamped her lips shut.

What was she going to say? That he broke her heart?

How was it that he'd been the one thrown into a spelled cage and yet he felt guilty?

The truck stopped. Tristan quickly argued, "I had no choice about leaving. I told you I was grabbed. They took me to South America and locked me in a spelled cage."

"The more I hear, the harder time I'm having accepting anything you say."

"I know, but it's true."

"You know what? I'm amazed at how little you care for anyone else. I suffered through your little trick the last time, but not again. If you were a supernatural being, it would be wonderful, because Kossman would pay dearly for–"

Tristan covered her mouth.

A jangling metal noise meant the lock was being opened.

He leaned down next to Mac's ear. "I know this sounds fantastical, but those two guys who grabbed us really are trolls. That means they're taking us to someone hunting for supernatural beings who will very likely be far more dangerous than your man Kossman."

Mac lifted her hand to his cheek and studied his face. "I never realized..."

"What?" Tristan asked cautiously, not sure what she was thinking.

"I never forgave you for making love to me, then, well, breaking my heart when I never heard from you again. I realize now that you couldn't help it, could you? You're delusional. I shouldn't have asked you to pretend, because it's real to you, isn't it? Try not to cause any trouble so they won't harm you while we wait on the ransom."

Tristan wanted to shake her, but not with her sore shoulder. He warned, "*Listen to me!* Don't let them know you're only human. They're probably looking for an Alterant right now and won't risk doing anything to either of us until they know for sure. I'm not delusional, but I am short of patience and too low on energy to trust my powers for a bit. I do have glowing eyes. I didn't pull a trick on you back then. I'm not removing these brown contacts until I feel stronger, but if you'll work with me, I'll get us out of this."

She shoved up until they were nose to nose. "You listen to me, Tristan. The media will get wind of this kidnapping because I live under a damn microscope as a Mackenzie, and they're already rabid to get another news flash out this week. If, once we're released, you start mouthing off that you're some kind of being with powers, I will strangle you myself. I'm willing to help you get mental counseling, but your eyes *do not* glow, for crying out loud. I need this job with Kossman. I will *not* see it go up in flames in the media because of a scam artist."

The door swung open with a loud whine.

Tristan dropped his head.

We're going to die painfully.

CHAPTER 5

Mac shook her head to clear her grogginess and untangle her thoughts. Where was she? Her mind did a replay up to the point of being ... kidnapped. Why?

Had to be for ransom.

Right?

Keeping her eyes closed, she listened for any hint of someone nearby. The longer they thought she was passed out, the longer they might leave her alone. Her arms ached. She'd expected to have her wrists bound, but she had what felt like manacles on her wrists and they'd been tied, or chained, above her head.

Manacles. This time her shiver had nothing to do with cold. This was just ... weird.

Had they asked Kossman about the ransom money? What if this wasn't about getting money out of a billionaire? What if this was about her being a Mackenzie?

That would be worse. Her brother would dance at her funeral.

Come to think of it, shouldn't the kidnappers have made her call someone for the money? Or did that only happen in the movies?

Preparing herself for whatever was going on, she lifted her head, expecting to find that she'd been locked in a room alone, with a guard watching her.

No guard, and not alone.

Tristan stood in the middle of the room.

No manacles. Not even tied up. Just him with his shirt off, and wearing only jeans. Good grief. What a body. Same light, tawny-colored hair, even though it was longer now and brushed his neck. Beefier body than before, and he'd been no wimp the last time. His face still had that sharp-angled, chiseled look though, with smooth skin she'd loved to touch again.

Strange, but she did miss the green eyes.

This was the worst time to be attracted to a lunatic, but seeing Tristan half-dressed reminded her of a happy memory.

When he'd pulled off his clothes in her bedroom.

He'd teased her. *Like what you see, Mac?*

She had loved what she'd seen. She'd met him during the last weeks of her first year at Georgia State. She'd gone there while waiting for her slot in the Titan scholarship program. Piedmont Park had been a two-mile walk from school, but only a few blocks from the attic apartment she rented over a garage.

She'd fallen for him in spite of his habit of wearing sunglasses everywhere. Ten days after they'd met, he'd kissed her and her world had tilted.

She'd had no idea about his habit of following her home each night to ensure she was safe. Then one night she felt the sharp tip of a knife against her back and froze.

The grunge-head would have succeeded in his attack if Tristan hadn't plowed into the guy so hard he actually went airborne a moment and hit a tree.

Until that point, any man in her life had been a threat to her. She hadn't expected one to step in to defend her.

By the time she had her wits about her, the guy was gone and Tristan convinced her the police would do nothing.

She'd thanked him and he'd told her to just go home.

Rude.

She'd walked across the lawn to her apartment and sat on the old steps leading up the side of the garage. He'd growled again at her to get inside.

It took a bit, but she convinced him to go upstairs with her.

When she woke up beside him the next morning, his sunglasses had slipped from his face. She lifted them, smiling while she studied him and waited for him to wake up.

He did.

Green eyes had glowed at her. *Glowed.*

That had sent her chasing a rare gene in her first year at Titan. One of her father's opponents for his first senate run had gone looking for weaknesses in Mackenzie's campaign, and paid another student to leak information on Mac. His contacts in the media taunted Mackenzie as the father of a woman hunting unicorns.

Brandon loved to remind his dad of the time when the future senator spent a buttload of money squashing the ridiculous story.

Mac would not deny her passion for ancient mythology, and had been known to attend Dragon Con. They grabbed onto all of it and made a mockery of her.

She still enjoyed Dragon Con. Screw those idiots.

But a lot had changed in five years.

Right now Tristan stared at her through muddy brown eyes that were as belligerent as the pose he struck, arms crossed and feet apart.

Why was he just standing there?

Could he see someone in the room that she couldn't?

This *had* to be a kidnapping for money. Kossman would pay, because he'd think she'd been captured with a nonhuman.

Kossman would break the bank for a nonhuman specimen.

Lucky for her, Tristan believed he was that special.

But even someone mental should be trying to escape.

She licked her dry lips and tried not to long for water. Speaking as softly as she could, and hoping Tristan would hear her, Mac said, "Is anyone else around?"

He shook his head.

"Why aren't you over here, trying to get my hands free so we can escape?" Yes, she'd like to believe Kossman would pay a ransom to get his employee and a potential specimen back, but she would be equally happy to escape without Kossman's help.

"They have me locked in an invisible cage."

She closed her eyes. *Oh, dear God.* How were they going to escape when Tristan had lost all touch with reality?

Opening her eyes, she started calculating. He had the brute strength with that body carved of muscle, but how could she get him to use those bulging guns if he believed trolls had captured them? What was next? Were they being held by an evil sorcerer?

Right.

Tristan had protected her once. Could she drag him back to reality by convincing him to do it again, then use that point of reality to get him to join up with her to escape? She asked, "How long have we been in here?"

"About two hours."

"What? I wouldn't have slept through all this for two hours."

"They used a spell to put you to sleep."

Argh! She held her patience. *Focus on the goal—getting out of here.* "Have they contacted Kossman?"

"No."

"Why not?"

"He's not behind the kidnapping. I heard one of them mention a sorcerer, but no name."

Of course. *Next he'll say he heard me thinking about an evil sorcerer.* She kept giving it the college try. "What are we going to do when they come back?"

"Depends."

She ground her jaw. "On?"

"If you'll do as I say. I'm not back to my full power, but I'm pretty sure I can take down two trolls. I just don't know who's really in charge."

Don't argue with someone mental. Damn him.

Tristan lowered his arms and looked to the right, where stairs led up to another floor. "Be quiet. They're coming."

She didn't hear anything. Another minute later, she caught the sound of footsteps heading down from a floor above. Was she in a basement?

A man in his early forties, with a shocking blue gaze and thick brown hair, came into view. He wore a nicely cut suit, similar to the one she'd seen him in yesterday.

Seth Kako.

Her nemesis. The man who was vying for the same position as Mac.

He didn't so much as pause as he passed Tristan, who glared daggers at Seth.

Tristan yelled, "What do you want with her when you have me, Sethos?"

Sethos? Did Tristan know him? She could forgive delusions, but not Tristan working with Seth.

Tristan pushed his hands, and strained like a mime pretending to shove a building off the foundation. Then he stopped and crossed his arms. Why did he have to be so gorgeous and so out of touch with the world?

Seth stopped in front of her and said, "You made a mistake signing on with Kossman, and now it's going to cost you. He'll be sad when he realizes you've disappeared after all he's done for you."

"What happened to Brewster and his man?"

Seth's eyes gleamed with pleasure. "Their van was righted and my men used a bit of majik I gave them. Brewster and his driver returned to Kossman, reporting that it was a bogus call, no glowing green eyes, and you told them you would see him on Monday. They'll also report that on the way back to the office they were in a hit-and-run wreck." Seth's smug voice had a sinister purr. "But don't get your hopes up, because you aren't going to be anywhere near Kossman come Monday."

Cold chills clawed their way up her spine.

There would be no ransom money sent for her. She warned, "What do you think Kossman will do when you show up without me? You don't think your prize specimen will talk and tell Kossman about me?"

"Him?" Seth jerked his thumb back toward Tristan, who was now quietly observing the conversation between her and Seth.

"Yes, him, unless you have someone else captive," she replied.

"I have no intention of taking Kossman *any* specimens. I only vied for the position because Kossman has the resources to flush out others like Tristan. But it appears I will now be the frontrunner for head of the department once you're *gone*."

She'd been kidnapped by a lunatic who was going to kill her for what boiled down to nothing more than a freaking job.

What was it about her that drew crazy men?

"You two know each other?" Tristan asked, sounding disgusted.

She leaned to her side to see past Seth and snapped, "Not as well as you two obviously know each other. You're clearly from the same psych ward as your buddy."

"He's not my damn buddy."

"Well it sounds pretty chummy to me. Or maybe you're the two best con artists to ever go after Kossman's money."

Seth raised his hands. "Children, children. Let's not argue. I have a witch who will pay well for you, Elaine." He turned to Tristan. "Much as I'd like to keep you, there's a Medb bounty on your head that I can't turn down."

Who or what is Mave?

Tristan laughed. "I hear there's a new witch council in Atlanta, and Rowan's at the head of it. Sure you want to get brought up on charges for dealing in humans?"

Mac knew enough from studying that there could be real witches, but the idea of trolls and sorcerers was ridiculous. Although, from the technical definitions she'd studied, a sorcerer, in ancient cultures, was basically considered to be a type of powerful witch. In spite of her circumstances, her curiosity kicked in.

Was there actually a witch council as Tristan claimed, or was he trying to scare Seth?

And what was the relationship between these two?

Were they scam artists who just knew each other, but did not work together?

Seth laughed at Tristan. "What the hell happened to your eyes? Do you even have any powers left, or did they strip them from you in Treoir? Heard you got stuck there after the Medb invasion."

Tristan shrugged. "Macha isn't known as a merciful goddess."

Mac's heart jumped in her throat. *We're back to glowing green eyes again?* Except Seth made it sound real.

Whatever was going on, Mac's survival instincts were not happy with her chances of leaving here alive. Worse, she might be handed over to someone who either *was* a witch or pretending to be one—how could she know for sure with Seth?—who apparently considered Mac valuable. As what? A sacrifice?

What would a witch do to me?

#

Tristan had tested the invisible walls imprisoning him. Sethos had him locked in tight.

And Sethos knew Mac.

But did Mac realize that Sethos was a sorcerer?

Had the bastard touched her?

The beast inside Tristan stirred at that thought. He ran the past few hours through his mind. Nope, Mac had no idea she'd been dealing with a predator. Hell, she *still* didn't believe Tristan and Sethos weren't human.

Sethos stepped close to Tristan's cage. If there had been no wall between them, Tristan could have grabbed him by the neck and snapped his head off.

When all else failed in Tristan's world, removing the head from the body usually did the trick.

Sethos glanced over at Mac then at Tristan. "How do you know Elaine?"

"Why? Worried I'll get word to Kossman?"

"No, there won't be anything left once I've enjoyed her and handed her off to the witch."

Tristan's beast raged inside him. "Touch her, and I'll take you apart one limb at a time. You know I can."

"Ah." Sethos smiled as though he'd just gained important information. "You two have slept together, huh? I will definitely keep her as entertainment for a while. It won't prevent the witch from paying top dollar."

Shit. Tristan wanted blood. *That's why you never get close to anyone.* The Medb coven had used his foster sister as leverage against him before, but Petrina was an Alterant who could protect herself.

Mac was human.

Sethos laughed all the way up the stairs and didn't even lock the door, so sure that he had Tristan contained.

Tristan had rested only a few hours. He could teleport himself out, but what about Mac?

Her head hung forward, as if she'd lost all hope.

Voices shouted upstairs, but sounded far off, like maybe outside the building. Power rocked the structure, and it shuddered. Someone shouted, *"Get the gryphon!"*

More bounty hunters. Would the suck ever quit hammering this day?

Mac hadn't moved. Her human ears weren't picking up on the threat heading their way.

Tristan and Mac had to leave. Now.

He couldn't risk his contacts hampering his powers. Tristan reached up and pinched each one off.

Closing his eyes, he teleported. When he opened his eyes, he stood next to Mac.

She jerked her head up at him. "What took you so long to do something?" Her mouth gaped open. "Glowing eyes again? Really, Tristan?"

Call him speechless. This was beyond fucked up.

The door burst open at the top of the stairs, and the sound of power being thrown around boomed.

"What's going on?" Mac cried out.

"They're having an auction for my head." He pointed his finger at her manacles, intending to unlock them with his kinetics. Nothing happened.

What the hell? He bet Sethos had put a spell on the lock that prevented it from opening except with the key.

She'd watched Tristan and her face fell at some realization. "You don't have superpowers. We need a key."

Loud explosions were going off upstairs, like someone had set fire to a fireworks plant.

While Mac's gaze was locked on the stairs, Tristan put his right hand on her shoulder to teleport both of them out. If she didn't know what was happening, she wouldn't freak out. He felt the change coming over him, but only half of him. When he looked at the left half of his body, it was slowly turning translucent.

Damn. He still couldn't teleport. Had Sethos warded this whole downstairs room?

Mac reached up and patted Tristan's hand then turned worried eyes to him. "Hide in that closet and I'll try to convince them you escaped through that high window."

Was she nuts? "First of all, we couldn't push a Chihuahua through that gap, and if I did hide where Sethos couldn't find me, he'd torture you."

She gave him a weak smile. "I can't get out. But you're free. If you can fight your way out, do it and call Kossman. He'll send in the equivalent of a SEAL team. I know he will. He's that kind of guy."

He's that kind of guy? Mac made Kossman sound like some kind of god.

What am I? Chopped liver? Tristan realized something else in her words. Mac was willing to help him escape even if she couldn't.

She'd do that for me?

Tristan didn't need a damn human to save Mac. He snarled, "I'm not leaving you."

Fighting poured down the stairs.

She argued, "Are you determined to get yourself killed?"

Tristan leaned down and kissed her hard. When he broke the kiss, he asked, "Would it matter?"

Her eyes warmed, then her heart climbed out and perched on her shoulder, just like it had five years ago.

He could see the truth in her gaze when she admitted, "Yes, it would matter. I must be just as delusional as the rest of you because,

God knows why, I still care about you."

"Hold that thought."

CHAPTER 6

Tristan turned around and stood between Mac and whatever was coming down the stairs.

Another explosion rocked the building, then Sethos yelled, *"Get the prisoners out of here!"*

Boots pounded down the stairs.

Sethos stopped short on the last step and stared at the middle of the room. Then his gaze cut over to where Tristan waited. "Nice trick, Alterant."

"I have others." Tristan smiled the way he had just before killing a witchdoctor who had entered his domain in South America with plans for using Tristan's blood. "Sounds like you just exhausted some of your powers, Sethos. You'd be wise to let us walk out of here. Do that and I won't kill you."

Not this time.

"You're not going anywhere, and we both know I can't allow her to live. So we're at cross-purposes."

Tristan shoved his hands forward and hit the sorcerer with a kinetic blast, knocking him back all the way to the far wall.

Sucka. Should have warded your body against my kinetics.

Sethos stumbled and shook it off. He snarled, "I don't have to deliver you undamaged." He rolled his hands around each other while he chanted, and a ball of fire bloomed in front of him. He threw the blazing ball at Tristan, who blocked it with kinetics.

If Sethos kept this up, he'd slowly drain Tristan's new burst of energy, but Tristan doubted he could kill the sorcerer with kinetics. Plus, he wasn't sure the majik he'd gained from that witch's cocktail last summer would be stronger than a powered-up sorcerer. A lot of things had happened since Tristan had last seen Mac, who'd thought he only had glowing eyes.

And as of tonight, that he was a psych ward deserter.

Sethos wound up his hands again to throw another flaming power ball.

Tristan realized what he could do. Using his kinetics again, he pointed at the ceiling and swiped his hand through the air. A thick conduit running through the exposed beams broke loose and yanked a power cable away from an electrical terminal.

Sethos looked up as the exposed hot wires on the cable hit him, lighting him up like a floodlight.

Darkness swamped the room, but without the contacts, plenty of light came through the small window for Tristan to see.

The troll who had carried Mac to this room and locked her in the manacles came running down the stairs. He dove at Sethos in an attempt to tackle him and break him away from the live wire. They both lit up before the troll's momentum broke the electrical connection.

Damn. Tristan had been hoping both of them would fry.

He pointed at the keys on the troll's belt and drew them to his hands.

Then he swung around to a white-faced Mac, unlocked her wrists, and eased down her arms that had to be aching. "Can you run?"

Her shocked eyes sharpened and met his. "Yes, but, um, you–"

He took off, towing her behind him. When he reached the stairs, the troll he'd stolen the keys from shoved up, growling like a pissed-off Rottweiler.

Tristan tossed a kinetic hit at him and sent the stocky bastard flying into metal cabinets. His body crushed them, then he dropped face-first to the floor.

Mac mumbled, "What the–"

Tristan pulled her up the stairs behind him before she could finish her question. At the top, he slowly looked around a corner and found the other troll's body with a burn hole through the middle. Next to him were two charred bodies he couldn't recognize.

Mac covered her nose. "What stinks?"

"Dead troll and–"

"What? Never mind."

He towed her through the great room, knocking lights out kinetically as he went. Pausing at the front door, he looked outside where the night was graveyard quiet.

Bad analogy.

She whispered, "What are you looking for?"

"Anyone and anything." He meant it. The woods could be full of bounty hunters who had found Sethos and might or might not know what he had inside. Sethos had been trafficking preternaturals, selling them as slaves and worse, for years. Tristan had barely avoided him more than once.

Sethos would recover soon.

Tristan had to get Mac as far from here as possible, but going out this door would leave them vulnerable to unknown threats.

That left him one choice, which he'd hoped to avoid. He squeezed Mac's hand. "Ready?"

"For what?"

It would probably be better not to tell her. "I have a place we can go that Sethos won't know about."

"But we don't know where we are to have any idea which way to run."

"We traveled for about an hour by truck, so we're twenty or thirty miles outside the Atlanta city limits."

"Okay, I'm ready."

Going on foot might be better if they could make it to the tree line sixty yards away. He had no idea if his misfire on teleporting downstairs had been due to Sethos placing some kind of ward on the room, or if it meant Tristan was still a quart low on power.

He turned to Mac and saw Sethos emerge from the stairs behind her.

She looked terrified, but asked in a firm voice, "How do you want to do this?"

Sethos sneered and cocked his arm to make a throw.

Tristan wrapped his arms around Mac, spun her, and called up all his power as heat struck his back.

CHAPTER 7

Mac had never suffered vertigo, but the world was spinning in a kaleidoscope of colors. She clutched Tristan and he groaned. Had she hurt him?

The spinning stopped and she took several breaths. "I was dizzy, but I'm good to go. You ready?" She lifted her head.

He looked down at her. "We're here."

"Where here?"

"A place I stay when I come to town."

She looked around at a room that reminded her of elegance from another era. The sleek furniture would now be called retro, with clean lines and linen upholstery. Lights glowed in the night outside, filtering through the sheers. She gawked at the room that she should not be standing in at this moment.

A bar stocked with fine liquor. Blonde hardwood floors ran across the space. She turned the other way. A six-foot-wide, flat-screen television sat in one corner.

"Mac?"

She pulled out of Tristan's embrace and walked to the window, pushing aside the sheer. The lights shining outside were from the Fox Theater marquee. Everything along the street had been decorated for the holidays. "Where are we?"

"Georgian Hotel in downtown Atlanta."

That's what she'd guessed, but hadn't wanted to believe. She turned back to Tristan. "How did we get here?"

"Teleported."

"Your eyes glow. You throw invisible power around and you teleport."

He nodded and crossed his arms. Waiting.

Did he expect her to keep calling him a lunatic? Of course he did, because earlier she'd thought if she kept saying it, she might make it true.

"What are you, Tristan?"

She grimaced at how she'd spoken to him. He hadn't flinched, but her question had sounded disdainful to her own ears. "I'm sorry, I didn't mean that to sound–"

"As if I'm some monster?" he finished. "I am. So is Sethos. So are a lot of people in this world you aren't supposed to know about."

She waited now, rather than say anything else insulting. Yesterday she would have backpedaled like crazy from this whole conversation, but she'd just traveled a great distance in a matter of seconds. And she'd watched Seth ... no, *Sethos* ... throw fireballs and Tristan shove kinetic energy around.

What would scientists who had studied kinetic energy for years give to have seen all that?

If Mac had learned one thing from facing difficult facts while growing up as a Mackenzie, it was that, ready or not, if truth stepped in front of you and stood there, you looked it in the eye and took it for what—or who—it was. Then you found a way to deal with it. You didn't try to make it go away, pretty it up, or dumb it down.

That had gotten her through accepting the truth when she'd learned about sharing DNA with the senator.

Tristan said, "I'm what's called an Alterant. There are ancient warriors who live among humans and protect them from people like Sethos. The majority of those warriors are called Beladors. You might say I'm ... associated with them."

"And what is Sethos?"

"He's a sorcerer."

"Seriously? Did you, I don't know, grab that from my thoughts?" A sorcerer. Her brain was going into overload.

"No, I can't read your mind." Tristan's lips curled into a sly grin for a moment, then his face and tone dropped back into serious zone. "Sethos captures preternatural creatures and sells them to the highest bidder, or hunts them down for a bounty for other beings who want to use them for dark purposes."

"Creatures ..." She cringed at that description and changed it. "I mean *beings* like you?"

"Yes. Like me."

She'd fallen for a quiet, wonderful man who had made her feel special when she knew she was no prize. The years had moved past since he disappeared, but not her longing to see him again even after reminding herself daily about how he'd made a joke of her.

At night, the Tristan she'd known for ten glorious days and one amazing night snuck into her dreams any time she closed her eyes.

And now, she knew the truth.

He hadn't played her false and walked. He'd been captured and locked away.

"Tristan, why were you locked up in South America?"

She saw him draw in a breath, watching her as he considered how to answer. His jaw worked. "It's complicated."

"Did you do something bad to deserve being locked up?"

"No."

Her heart had known the answer, but her brain needed her to ask and hear it with her own ears just the same.

"Alterants have never been understood, and at the time, some considered us dangerous, which we are, but I was locked up because of fear–on the chance that I *might* do harm. Not because I did."

How horrible.

She couldn't imagine what it had been like, forced to live alone in a jungle. And even when he thought she'd caused his imprisonment and that she'd been behind his capture tonight, he still stepped between her and danger. Why would he do that after all this time?

She considered all he'd said and mused, "You're a ... Belador?"

"No. Well, sort of. Like I said, I'm an Alterant. That means I have half Belador blood and half Medb."

"Mave?" She'd heard that earlier. The question must have shown on her face.

He spelled it for her and explained, "The Medb are a coven of powerful dark witches, ruled by a goddess who calls herself Queen Maeve and has been around as long as our goddess."

This just got better and better. "You have a goddess?"

"I don't personally claim her, but the Beladors answer to Macha, and so do the Alterants for now, only because it's better than being stuck with Queen Maeve." He swiped a hand across the stubble on his jaw. Now that she took the time to notice, he looked exhausted. Throwing power around and teleporting must really take it out of a guy.

Tristan walked to her and started to reach out, then dropped his hand. "It's a long story."

"I studied about those goddesses and—" What was she trying to say? That she believed *all* of this? How could she not, after what she'd just experienced?

Tristan put his hands on her shoulders. "I know this is a lot to take in."

"Goddesses, Beladors, Alterants, trolls and ... you say Seth Kako is a sorcerer."

#

Tristan could call Sethos a lot of things, but he'd go with sorcerer for now. Mac had absorbed a lot already. "He's a very nasty one. His real name is Kakosethos. Greek for *Sethos the Mean*." Heat still singed Tristan's back. It hurt like a son of a bitch, but he wanted to make sure Mac wouldn't go screaming out of here while he called up his beast power to heal himself.

She sniffed. "What's that singed smell?"

"Sethos got in a last shot at me as we left."

"Where?"

"My back. If you won't freak out, I can heal–"

"Let me see." She hurried behind him. "Oh my God, Tristan. Your back has a hole in it. You're burned. You need a hospital."

"No." He swung around and caught her shoulders again, gently, to anchor her. "Human doctors can't fix me. I need a shower."

"It's. A. *Hole*," she said slowly, as if she still thought he was an idiot. "A big, freakin', *burned* hole!" she shouted at him.

"I can heal it."

"Are you crazy? No, that looks insanely bad." She kept trying to pull away to get around to his back again.

Unbelievable. Mac had accepted Tristan fighting nonhumans, that his glowing eyes were real, and teleporting, taking it all in stride, but she freaked out over a wound.

His wound. Damn, that caused a warm spot in his chest.

When was the last time anyone had fussed over him?

Let me think. Never.

"Mac, listen to me. I've got this. Really." He let her go.

She stepped back with her arms crossed and a determined look in her eyes. "You could be dying while we argue."

"I'm not dying." He couldn't explain any more. He was physically wiped out from flinging all that power around. This constant drain would screw his getting back up to full speed.

Ah shit. And how was he going to take Petrina and Bernie back to Treoir on time if he didn't have enough energy to teleport even one of them by tomorrow? "Damn it."

"What?"

"Nothing." Once Tristan had Mac safe, he'd figure out about taking those two back to Treoir. He might have to send them without him. Even so, he'd need time between each teleport.

A shower would clear his head, then he'd have to shut down for a while to have any chance of killing a light kinetically without help.

Tristan strode to the bathroom, tugging his shirt up as he walked, but the material stuck and pulled at his skin. He growled a curse. Material must have melted.

"Stop, Tristan!"

He paused and Mac blew past him.

She ordered, "Follow me."

Amused with her take-no-prisoners tone, he followed her into the bedroom and on to the bathroom.

She peeled off her sweater and jeans, then stepped inside the glass shower and cranked on the jets. Water hit all the exposed skin that her bra and panties, pink, no less, didn't cover.

Not what he'd had in mind, but the horndog in him was on board.

She turned to him, holding the door open. "Take off everything but your shirt and get in here."

He normally didn't like bossy women.

Evalle Kincaid annoyed the piss out of him when she got mouthy and started tossing around demands. His sister Petrina could be just as irritating when she got her back up.

But demanding Mac was a serious turn-on. And that right there was why men dropped half their brain cells every time they dropped their pants around a woman.

By the time he'd shucked his jeans and stepped into the shower, he was hard and throbbing.

Water poured over Mac, turning her into his own personal wet dream nymph.

She glanced down to find him erect and poised for her.

Was she impressed? No. She arched an eyebrow at him. "Turn around."

"Isn't that my line?"

"Do it."

He did and water sprayed across his raw skin. "*Shit!*"

Way to kill a hard-on. But fuck that hurt.

"Don't be a baby." She gently tugged the material as it softened under the water and pulled away. She murmured encouraging words the whole time, which did little to ease the feeling of his skin being ripped from his back.

"It's clean, and the material is out of the wound," she finally announced. "What are we going to do now, superhero?"

She had a mouth on her.

"Just stand back," he said, keeping his back to her while he propped one arm against the tiled wall to hold himself upright. His knees had almost buckled while the water battered the raw wound.

Searching inside, Tristan called on his beast, which came slowly to life. Not all the way to shifting, but enough to send healing power to his back. Over the next few minutes, muscle regenerated, and a layer of skin formed. Must have closed the wound, because the water no longer felt like tiny daggers. He'd be sore, but he could deal with that.

The showerhead stopped spewing water.

When he turned to Mac, she had her hand over her mouth and her eyes were open so wide he could see white all around.

He swallowed, but what had he thought? That she'd forgotten he was a monster?

There was no way he'd ever be just a normal man to her again.

Not a human male like ... fucking Kossman.

Thinking of her boss just pissed Tristan off. The son of a bitch had sent her out into danger if he really believed in supernaturals. Anyone in the preternatural world had heard of Kossman, who was richer than four feet up a bull's ass. Women whispered about him being sex on a stick.

Even Mac had Kossman on a pedestal.

When Tristan hadn't been able to unlock her shackles, she'd implored him to escape and call Kossman. *He'll send the equivalent of a SEAL team.*

She'd never think of Tristan the way she clearly idolized Kossman. A mere human.

The one thing Tristan would never be.

He didn't want anyone to idolize him. But standing here, looking at Mac in all her gorgeous wet glory, he wanted her to look at him the way she had the night he'd saved her from a mugging. And the way she'd stared up at him as he'd driven into her when they'd made love.

The way she'd looked at him when they first met in the park, as a man ... not a monster.

She hadn't cared about anything but him during those moments. As far as she'd known, he was just another guy.

Just a normal human guy.

Until he'd met her in Piedmont Park, he'd had few women in his life and none he'd wanted to ever see again. Certainly not a woman he'd burned for the way he'd wanted Mac.

And still did.

Time to put that all in the past and leave it there.

He was as bad as Bernie for wanting a human woman. Not an option in his world, with his life being pulled between the Beladors and the Medb.

But for just this moment, Tristan wanted to taste her again and feel the peace that had come over him during their one night together.

She cleared her throat. "Five years ago, when you disappeared ... would you have left me like that if you hadn't been grabbed?"

"No." He stepped over to her. "I thought about walking away the night you invited me up to your apartment. I didn't want to risk anyone seeing my eyes, especially you."

"What stopped you from leaving?"

He took his time answering. Should he tell her the truth or give her another reason to run from him?

Mac didn't run. She deserved the truth.

He said, "You. I couldn't leave because I wanted you too much to let you go."

She stared and stared until he accepted his lot in life. He shouldn't have made love to her back then without telling her he was not human. Now she knew. He had no excuse this time, which meant he'd get her to safety, and then disappear.

Tristan couldn't take the silence anymore. "You can say what you're thinking. How could I have touched you without telling you I'm a monster?"

Her tongue slid over her pink lips, torturing him with yet another vision he'd never forget.

She stepped up and put her hand on his cheek. "You're not a monster, Tristan. I grew up with monsters, human ones. You have the ability to heal. That's a gift, not a curse. You're the most honorable man I've ever met, and I don't regret one minute of our night together. I just want to know one thing."

"What?" His voice came out sounding like a rusty hinge.

"Do you still want me?"

CHAPTER 8

"Tristan?"

His brain finally caught up to Mac's words and shook him back to the here and now. Did he still want her?

Tristan didn't waste the time telling Mac *hell yes.*

He covered her mouth with his, running his hands through her hair, and pulling her to him.

She lunged into the kiss. If it got any hotter in here, they'd set the room on fire. Her arms wrapped around his neck as if she feared he'd let go.

Not a chance.

He hoisted her up to his hips and she hooked her legs around him, sealing his aching hard-on between them. Tristan pointed a finger at the shower door and it opened. He stepped out and set her on the marble sink.

Her hands moved across his shoulders and gripped the backs of his arms. The woman was a tiger in bed ... and on a sink.

His tongue met hers and danced an erotic rhythm.

Now that his hands were free to roam, he turned them loose. His fingers went straight to her breasts where he unclipped her bra. *Love those front clasps.* Two beautiful mounds filled his hands. He squeezed gently and flicked a finger across each hardened tip.

She clenched her legs that were still around him. "Yes, yes, yes!"

He could smell her desire and eased his way down, kissing one breast as he tortured the other with his fingers. Drawing the nipple into his mouth, he nipped it.

She gasped and shuddered.

He kissed the spot and moved down her abdomen, loving every inch with his mouth. When he reached her panties, he pulled them off and settled in to enjoy the pleasure he'd missed all these years.

Mac's heart thundered in her chest and the world turned into an erotic kaleidoscope. How had she lived all these years without his touch?

An Alterant. She'd ask him more about that later. Right now, she had her own superhero lover.

Tristan's fingers gripped her bare legs and slid his hands around to her inner thighs, gently opening her. One finger brushed through her curls and damp heat.

Then it moved away.

She fought the urge to cry. It had been too long for her, and she wanted to feel everything now. Her voice trembled. "Don't ... stop."

"I won't."

Anticipation coiled inside her, waiting for his touch. When his tongue swept across the bundle of nerves screaming for release, she lifted off the sink.

He held her down and suckled her.

She'd met no one—no man—she could trust enough to open herself this way. Not in the last five years. It took only seconds for all that longing to coil tightly, then for the release to explode through her. Every part of her body felt charged with energy.

When she finally stopped shaking, Tristan had her up against his chest, holding her and kissing her face and hair. She pulled back and looked into his beautiful eyes.

Green was officially her favorite color. "I missed you."

He closed his eyes and dropped his forehead to hers. "Thank you."

"For what?"

Lifting his head, he kissed her sweetly. "Missing me. Wanting me. Letting me make love to you."

"I think I should be thanking you, since I'm the one who's limp as a noodle right now," she teased.

"I'm not done." An unholy look glowed in his eyes.

"Then get to it."

He laughed and it was music to her ears. "I *have* missed that mouth of yours."

She'd seen him smile, but hearing him laugh, so honest and real, caused her heart to squeeze. He kissed her again and she had no doubt about his lusty intentions. She said in a mock-diva tone, "Still waiting on the final act ... unless you're still too weak from throwing all that ... power ... stuff ... around."

He grabbed her head and forced it back, his lips an inch from hers. "You're hot when you're bossy."

Grinning, she said, "I'll keep that in mind."

"I'll wipe that smile off your face as soon as I bury myself deep inside you."

"Keep talking like that and I'll come again ... *oh, wait!*"

"What?"

"No condoms."

Tristan arched an eyebrow and gave her an all-knowing smirk. "There better be one in here or I'm going to be very disappointed in my friend who loans this place to me." He waved his hand at a drawer that was just out of reach.

The drawer opened, and with a flick of his finger, a condom flew up to his open palm. He sheathed himself and lifted Mac back into his arms.

Once her legs locked around him, she shifted up and down against him.

Tristan growled. "You don't want to tease the beast."

He backed her up against the bathroom door. She put a hand on his chest and waited until their gazes met to tell him, "When we're together, it's only you and me. I don't see a beast. I see a man I can't wait to feel inside me, stroking over and over until–"

"Fuck." He lifted her onto him and slid home in one stroke.

She felt that all the way to her nipples and sucked in a breath. He stroked again and again, picking up momentum.

She bit his shoulder and he buried himself deeper, releasing a loud groan. Nipping and licking behind her love bites, she kissed his salty skin and whispered, "Harder."

He answered her demand and she clawed his back, clenching against his sweet assault. When he came it was with a shout that sounded primal and fierce, pounding away and sending her over with him. Moments later, he held her pinned against the door as he heaved hard breaths in and out.

She hung, draped across his damp body. "I'm done. Stick a fork in me."

He chuckled. "You say the damndest things."

Tensing, she asked, "Is that good or bad?"

"Better than good. Don't ever change."

She smiled. Everyone else thought she was a bubble off of center. But Tristan got her. Her heart did a happy dance.

Now, how would they go forward from here?

What could she tell Kossman?

CHAPTER 9

Tristan sensed something off. He slowly opened his eyes, searching the room then taking stock of the bed he was sprawled over. He had a mouth-watering body lying across his chest.

That's right ... he was in the human world, not on Treoir.

He relaxed, content to listen as Mac's chest rose and fell with gentle breaths.

His hands would not stay away from her. He stroked her back, moving the sheet to her waist. That's all it took to be hard again. He wanted more of last night. Resting hadn't been on the agenda, even after a second round of steaming sex in the shower.

Her fault. She'd wanted to shower again.

She stirred and lifted her head, looking only at him.

He waited for her to flinch at seeing his eyes again.

Not Mac. She smiled and said, "Tell me something special about your powers that no one else can do."

He thought on it, comparing different abilities. "I'm not sure if this is unique to Beladors, but I've never heard of any other preternatural group that can link with each other."

"What do you mean?"

"This is another thing that's hard to explain, but we reach out and join our power to another Belador. Once we do, we have more power as a team."

"Wow, that's amazing."

"Unless someone in the link is killed," Tristan clarified.

"Why? What happens then?"

"Everyone linked dies." And that was only one reason he hadn't experimented much with linking. He'd done it a couple of times and survived, but the Alterants had not, as a rule, been groomed to fight as a team.

"That sucks." Mac jumped from one topic to the next. "Can you see at night?"

"Better than night vision."

"Oh, that's going to make sex on the beach fun during summer. We can go anywhere after dark."

If only his life were that simple. He couldn't stay with her. He wanted to turn his back on everyone and everything to stay right here. Life didn't work that way.

He started thinking of what he needed to do to make sure she was safe once he left. His chest hurt just thinking about letting go of her.

Stroking her hair, he smiled at her happy expression. "Are you ever unhappy?"

Her face fell.

Way to ruin her good mood, asshole. "What'd I say?"

"You didn't do anything wrong, so stop trying to take the blame."

Did he do that? He'd been blamed for so much over the years it came naturally to assume he was at fault. "Okay, if I didn't do it then what made you sad?"

"I've had my moments of being unhappy. I was miserable growing up in the lap of luxury, or at least everyone thinks I lived in luxury. My father and brother are ... they're difficult. I've struggled since striking out on my own, but I've been happy even when making ends meet has been tough. I will admit you made me sad when you left, but I thought you'd played me for a fool then you were done with me."

"Baby, you're nobody's fool. I'm sorry about what happened."

"Yes, but you spent five years in hell thinking I'd turned you over to the demon police."

Demon police. More Mac talk. He lifted her hair, twisting it around his fingers. "That's in the past. Now we need to figure out how to make sure you're safe before I leave."

She shot up, shoving her hands hard on his chest. "You're leaving? Again?"

Tristan pushed up on his elbows. "I have to go back to another realm. My foster sister is here and so is another Alterant. We aren't supposed to leave Macha's realm."

"Then what are the three of you doing here? I mean, I'm thrilled you're back, but I'm so confused."

He was, frankly, amazed at how well she'd handled everything, and owed her any explanation he could give her. "Macha doesn't want us to leave her realm and, as you've seen, there are groups hunting us. She doesn't know that I can teleport. I'm the only one of our group who can, so I've been bringing each Alterant home to the human world for a visit during the holidays, then taking them back two days later."

"Where is this realm?"

Tristan scratched a day's growth of beard. "That's going to be tough to explain. It's Treoir Island, home of Treoir Castle, and all of that is hidden in a mist above the Irish Sea. But, no, you couldn't see it if you flew over the Irish Sea."

"When will you be back?"

"I don't know. We're waiting on a decision from a Tribunal made up of three gods and goddesses." Yep, this sounded bizarre even to his ears. "There's no guarantee that they'll approve our petition to be a recognized race. If not ..." He shrugged.

She cocked her jaw, thinking hard on something then she snapped her fingers. "We should tell Kossman. If he knew about you, surely he'd want to protect Alterants."

Kossman again.

"No." Tristan set her to the side of him. "The less humans know about us, the better for both sides." He paused and debated on asking something. No way to ask and not sound like an ass, but old suspicions died hard when you'd been through all that he had. He had to know. "You said last night that you needed to hand a supernatural being to Kossman to gain the position Sethos is also after. Is that why you want me to stay?"

She stood and grabbed the sheet, wrapping it around her. "How can you ask me that?"

He cringed internally beneath her stern gaze, but the past still had a hold on him and probably always would. Allowing feelings to influence where to place his trust had come with a painful price in the past. He'd been sold to a witch because he'd been born a freak. That's where he'd met Petrina. The day that witch attacked Petrina, he'd shifted into a beast and killed the bitch.

Over the years, he'd tossed out all kinds of stories about being in multiple foster homes, but the truth was, his mother hadn't wanted a monster. Until he'd met Mac, every woman Tristan had been around had tried to screw him over, except for Petrina.

Dammit, he was a blunt asshole, but that personality flaw had saved him a lot of trouble in the past. Still, he should've thought twice before being so crass with Mac.

He shoved up off the bed and stood in front of her. "I just want that out on the table so I know."

"Here's your answer. If you have to ask, then what I say wouldn't matter. I don't know what other women have done to you in the past, but I'm not judging you by the men in my past so don't judge me by those women. I don't need you as a trophy."

Good goddess, he'd managed to piss her off royally. "Mac."

She backed up a step, tugging the sheet with her. "You know what? You're leaving anyhow, so go back to your realm. If I see you again, I do. If I don't, well, I'll know I was too much effort."

"Mac."

She lifted a hand to silence him and stepped back. "I spent five years learning how to accept being left behind. I know you didn't do it on purpose, but it was still ... painful. I'm glad you're safe and I'm glad I know what you are, but you're leaving again and you still don't trust me. Let's not make this any more difficult than it is."

I really am some kind of dickhead to screw this up. He started to apologize and Bernie's voice reached him telepathically.

Tristan, are you there?

Tristan lifted a hand to ask Mac to give him a moment, then he replied to Bernie. *I'm here. What's up?*

I only have sixty seconds so don't interrupt. Sethos has Petrina and me. He says he'll trade us for a woman named Elaine Mackenzie and if you don't bring her within an hour, he'll give Petrina to the Medb, then take me to some Kossman dude and tell him that Elaine is trying to sell us to a higher bidder. This Sethos is whacked.

Where are you?

Sethos has us bound and has Petrina levitated over a pit full of blades. One can cut her body in half. Bernie finally spouted out directions then warned Tristan, *You know this is a trap, but I can't save your sister without your help.*

Tell Sethos I'm coming and if either of you is harmed, I'll make him beg for death.

I'll tell him, but he's–

Bernie's voice disappeared.

Tristan tried to reach out to Bernie, then Petrina, and hit a barrier.

Sethos had them warded against telepathy.

Mac had quieted and watched him with trepidation. "What's going on?"

"Bernie's my friend who got away last night when your two men grabbed me. He just called me telepathically to tell me Sethos has found him and my sister, Petrina. Sethos is offering a trade. You for them. I'm taking you to Kossman, and he better keep you safe while I'm gone."

"No. I'm going with you."

"To be sacrificed?"

"Can you call them again, telepathically?"

Tristan shook his head. "Sethos must have a ward blocking our communication."

She rolled her eyes and muttered, "Wards. Telepathy. Unicorns will be next."

Tristan wanted to chuckle at her, but worry chewed at his gut. "I have to go, Mac. I only have an hour to reach them."

"Can we teleport?"

"I'm going to borrow Otto's van. He's a silent partner who keeps this place for me. I need to conserve my energy. Teleporting isn't a natural gift, and it drains me every time. I can't go into this low on power."

"Then we'd better get showered and dressed. Call your friend Otto. Who is he, or is this a *what is he* question?"

"He's a troll."

She looked appalled. "I thought they were bad."

"Some are and some aren't. Just like humans aren't all good or bad."

"Oh." She grabbed two fists of hair and shook her head and muttered, "I'm going to need a program to keep up with the players."

Tristan lifted the hotel phone and told Otto what was up then announced, "The van will be out front in two minutes."

She grumbled, "Showering is out. Me and you naked takes way more than two minutes."

Tristan pulled her to him and kissed her as long as he could, finally breaking away to say, "I'm sorry for being a jackass." He watched her for any sign that he'd pushed her too far. "Are we good?"

Her eyes glistened at his final two words, then her lips eased into a smile that grew into a grin. "Yes. Lucky for you that you're a superhero in bed."

How could a man not be crazy over this woman? "Damn straight." He kissed her again then took a leap and gave her one more hit of truth. "I don't want to leave you."

"That's the first right thing you've said since waking up, which wipes away that whole stupid comment about me handing you over to Kossman."

It was going to take a bit to change his mindset, but for Mac he was willing to accept that she was exactly what she seemed to be.

A sweet, honest woman.

Ignoring the come-get-me look in her eyes, which should earn him a freaking award, Tristan ordered, "Get dressed. I'm going to have Otto drop you off on the way."

"You can't do that."

"Why?"

"Because I have an idea." She sashayed off, picking up clothes as she went. "But it's not for free. You're going to help me get a Christmas tree home."

Christmas tree? She was certifiable. "You're still not going, Mac."

"You are so sexy when you get all badass," she called from the bathroom.

This woman will be the death of me.

CHAPTER 10

Tristan led Mac down a trail that kept descending through Kennesaw Mountain National Battlefield Park, listening and watching for anything that didn't belong here. Mac was no pushover, but he wished she had on armor instead of jeans and the wool coat Otto, his troll friend, had loaned her. She walked along in hiking boots, silent as a ghost, just as Tristan had instructed her.

Soft puffs of frosted air slipped from her lips on each exhale. She glanced up, sweet hazel eyes brimming with trust twisting his insides. He had to keep too many people safe.

What if he failed?

She winked at him.

Mac had badgered him until he finally accepted that he had only one choice. That didn't mean he was happy about it.

Sleet hit him in the face and neck. He'd opted to wear a thick sweatshirt for ease of movement, and for shifting.

If it came to that.

The weather had been deteriorating for the half hour it took to drive from downtown Atlanta to this northwest corner of the metro area. With the wet and cold expected to only get worse, no one jogged or walked past them on trails normally busy with foot traffic.

All at once, the sleet stopped and everything went very still.

No sound of even a small animal moving through the dead leaves and sticks carpeting the ground beyond the path.

The lack of natural activity confirmed for Tristan that they were nearing Sethos.

If that bastard had hurt Petrina or Bernie, Tristan would let his beast off the leash and shred Sethos.

The chunky troll who worked with the sorcerer stepped onto their path.

Tristan forced his hands to stay down and not blast him through the woods. The troll took one look at Mac's wrists handcuffed in front of her, and nodded, then turned away to lead them off the trail and through briar-infested thickets that bit at their clothes.

When Tristan emerged from the woods with Mac beside him, he stepped into an open area that would be a nice place to run a dog and throw Frisbees. That's what humans did here.

Sethos stood next to Bernie, who had his hands and ankles bound with a rope linked between them. Petrina had been contained the same way, but she floated horizontally over an open pit.

The sharp tips of ten blades extended just above the pit. One wide blade was positioned right below her neck.

With her back facing down, Petrina had no chance to use kinetics to survive if Sethos released the levitation majik.

Tristan tried to reach them telepathically but he hit a mental wall again. The ward.

He ordered the troll, "Go tell your master I won't trade unless I can speak to my people. I brought his package unharmed. I want the same assurance."

The troll waddled over and, halfway to Sethos, blue light shimmered around him as he stepped through the ward.

Now Tristan knew where the barrier was.

He didn't want to do this, didn't like any part of it, but Mac made a good point. If Tristan died trying to rescue Petrina and Bernie, everyone would lose, including her.

Sethos said, "No."

That came through clearly, so Tristan replied, "Have it your way. I'll hand Elaine over to Kossman, and then I'm coming after you with everything VIPER and the Beladors have." Tristan fought the urge to roll his eyes at the absurdity of that statement.

VIPER would cut him down where he stood and Macha would have her say in an hour if he was lucky enough to get Petrina home, but Sethos didn't need to know any of that. Bernie wouldn't make it, but Tristan would return to be with him.

"You can see them," Sethos argued.

He must want Mac bad. Tristan said, "Then let me talk to them. That's the only way I'll know they're okay. Do that, and we have a deal."

Sethos considered that a moment, then made some sound of

concession. He said, "I'll allow you thirty seconds to speak. Then we make the trade. One stupid move and Petrina gets skewered. The Medb say that some of the Alterants regenerate if they're in gryphon form, but I doubt it works if the head is removed."

Waving his hand and murmuring words, Sethos finished his chant and nodded at the troll.

Tristan yelled, "Time doesn't start until you take the gags off their mouths." Then he shoved a telepathic order at Bernie and Petrina. *This is Tristan. Both of you link with me now.*

Sethos snarled, "You can hear them grunting. That's enough. Send me Elaine."

"Not until I hear my sister and Bernie speak." Tristan sent another blast. *Link, dammit!*

We're trying, Petrina shouted in Tristan's head.

Mac started to move and Tristan pulled the chain hooked to her waist tight, buying the few seconds he needed for Petrina and Bernie to link. "What are the Medb doing with Alterants, Sethos?"

"Making me a rich man for any that I bring them."

The Alterants Tristan knew hadn't practiced linking and he'd only done it once with Evalle. That hadn't turned out so well.

But he felt sure Petrina could do it.

Sethos complained, "Your time is running out."

"Or yours is. Just depends on how you look at it," Tristan shrugged, acting unconcerned, which deserved an Oscar considering that his neck was clammy with panic. This would end soon and with blood spilled.

Tristan just didn't want it to be the blood of the three he had to keep safe.

Petrina lifted her chin, and in that instant Tristan felt her energy reach inside him and clamp onto his power, doubling his strength.

Tristan urged, *Come on, Bernie. Reach out to my power.*

Sweat poured down Bernie's face with the effort of clearly trying to do something he couldn't figure out.

Sethos said, "Time's up. Send Elaine over or we're done."

Mac pulled around and shook her fists at Tristan, yelling, "What are you waiting for? You tricked me and now you're going to just hand me over to some *psychopath!* Might as well get it done so I never see your miserable hide again." Her eyebrows shot up in a what-is-the-hold-up look?

"He's not all that bad, are you, Sethos?" Tristan held a calm mask throughout her verbal thrashing, but roared telepathically, *Petrina, grab Bernie's power!*

Turning to the troll, Sethos said, "You watch these two. I'm going after Elaine."

Petrina's telepathic voice finally said, *Got him!*

Tristan shouted, *"Now!"*

Sethos spun around, and stared at Tristan, distracted. Perfect.

Energy like he'd never experienced surged inside Tristan's chest and flowed through his limbs. He reached out with his power and teleported Bernie and Petrina, but not to him. He sent them to the parking lot where Otto waited with the van, ready to free them from the bindings.

Tristan enjoyed the moment of disbelief in the sorcerer's eyes at losing his bargaining chips.

Sethos lifted off the ground and flew at them. When he hit the ward, a flash of blue bloomed then vanished.

Tristan shoved up a kinetic wall to block the attack and knocked Sethos backwards. He warned, "Don't ever touch anyone who belongs to me again, Sethos. And, if you're smart, you'll leave this area now. I have a feeling VIPER will receive a report of a sorcerer dealing in both nonhumans *and* humans in this region."

Pulling himself together, Sethos settled his feet on the ground and countered in a calm tone. "You win this round, Alterant. Count yourself fortunate, but don't think you'll be so lucky a second time."

"It's not luck. You show your face again and my luck will turn you inside out. Literally."

Tristan glanced at Mac, who jerked her hands apart with the showmanship of a magician and the chains fell away, just as he'd tutored her. She smiled and said, "See? No bloodshed."

Mac took a step toward Tristan.

Sethos called out a curse.

Mac jerked around to look at the crazy sorcerer.

Everything slowed to microseconds as Tristan twisted toward Sethos, who lifted his hands in the air and called on gods of darkness.

Tristan felt power lash out and wrap his kinetic wall, turning it into black glass then shattering it.

Sethos whipped his arm down, throwing an arc of blazing energy at Tristan.

Face rocked with horror, Mac dove between Sethos and Tristan.

CHAPTER 11

Tristan's world spun back into action at the speed of light.

When Mac launched her body toward his, Tristan grabbed her to shove her around behind him.

But the power and curse Sethos released struck Mac just as she reached Tristan. Her body spun away before he could grasp her. She landed on the ground in a silent heap.

Tristan howled and unloaded everything he had for power, slamming kinetic blasts at Sethos and shooting arcs of energy from his eyes. He'd done that once before in the jungle, and had no idea he still could.

Sethos flipped up and backwards in the air, somersaulting to land on his feet. As he did, he whipped a flaming arc from each hand at Tristan, who batted them away with kinetic slaps.

The troll hurried over and lifted Mac to carry her off.

Tristan couldn't fight on two fronts. With the combined power from Bernie and Petrina, Tristan called up his beast and exploded out of his body and clothes, growing ten feet in two breaths.

He teleported next to Sethos, who had no time to react before Tristan grabbed him with the giant eagle beak of a gryphon, snapping his body in half. He threw the parts down and stomped on them, blood spraying in all directions.

Nothing would put that bastard back together.

Tristan extended a lion's paw that could club a grizzly bear and pointed one claw at the troll trying to steal Mac. He lifted the troll off the ground with a kinetic power Tristan had never before experienced and turned the bastard in mid-air.

The damn troll growled and lifted Mac's leg to take a bite.

With a flip of Tristan's other paw, he yanked Mac out of the troll's grasp. She flew to him. Tristan caught her rigid body and cradled her with his huge wing. Using his powers, he spun the troll around and bashed him into the ground headfirst, once, twice, then a third time.

If he lived, Otto could have him.

Tristan laid Mac gently on the ground. He drew his body back into his human form and conjured something to wear. All he got was a pair of shorts. Guess his power was too depleted for real clothes.

She hadn't even blinked.

He dropped to his knees. "Talk to me, Mac."

She grunted something that might be, "Can't."

What the hell had Sethos done to her?

Tristan touched her neck. She was cold as ice. Deathly cold. He shoved her sweater up. White veins crept along her chest and the skin had started turning gray. He lifted her blouse. Shit. The veins were thickening around her heart. Her eyes moved to his, pleading with him.

Her lips were turning blue.

He put his hand on her chest and tried to send his power through his fingers. She jerked and he stopped.

What good is this power if I can't even save a human?

She reached up and covered his hand.

The white veins started crawling up his arm. Her eyes registered alarm and her heart beat faster beneath his hand. The damn veins began spreading more quickly.

Had his touch caused that?

He tried to lift his hand. Couldn't. It was bound to her chest.

You have the ability to heal. That's a gift, not a curse.

He didn't know if he heard Mac thinking that or if it was only something he remembered her saying earlier.

Staring deep into her eyes, Tristan started calling up his beast's healing powers to shove the venom out of *his* body.

The lines stopped moving.

Her eyes rolled up, showing white.

Tristan lifted his head and bellowed, *"No majik will take her from me!"* But he was losing her. He could feel her heart slowing down. Where was the majik he'd gotten from the witch's brew?

Closing his eyes, he searched inside for his power, and words began scrolling rapidly through his mind. He forced them to slow down.

Darkness grows where light is weak. Light to light, mind to mind, two as one will freedom find.

He whispered the words until they took control of him. He repeated them, louder and louder, until a noise broke through his mad shouting.

"Tristan?"

He looked down to where Mac's fingers were clutching his arm. Her face had returned to a healthy, bright pink color and the white veins were gone.

Tristan grabbed her to him and she groaned, "Still sore."

He eased his hold. "Sorry, baby. Thought I'd lost you."

"No chance in hell." She turned to his face and kissed him. When she stopped, she said, "Took me too long to find you again."

He kissed her again just because he needed it right then. If his life were his own, he'd be bundling her up and taking her back to keep tucked away at his place in the city. He nuzzled her neck. "What were you thinking?"

"That he was going to kill you."

She'd put her life before his. "I can take a hit. You're a human."

She leaned back and gripped his shoulders. "I may only be human, but I'm tough. I won't stand by when you're attacked."

Where had this woman come from, and why did he have to give her up?

Petrina's voice interrupted the moment. *Tristan, are you okay?*

Yes.

Bernie says we have to get back to Treoir.

Heading back to you now. Tell Otto we need cleanup down here.

You got it, bro.

Tristan got Mac to her feet. "I've got someone coming to clean this up. Let's head back."

"You have no clothes on."

Taking her hand, he headed to the trail. "It's enough. With my metabolism, this feels cool, not icy. But you're cold, and probably going through shock."

"After being threatened with death by witch, and watching you throw invisible thunderbolts and teleport, a crazy sorcerer and his vicious troll are nothing. Almost dying by a spell did give me pause, but I'm all better now that I've had your Alterant healing."

He shook his head at her sarcasm.

She stopped, waiting on him to look back before she said, "Thank you for saving my life."

"You should be cursing me for putting you in danger."

"You didn't do that, Tristan. Stop taking blame for everyone else's decisions. I chose to try for the lead position with Kossman."

Reminding him of that sobered him. Tristan tugged on her, and they continued another twenty steps and found the short trail back to the parking lot. The clock fought him with each minutes sliding away. He didn't have time to fix that problem and get Bernie and Petrina back to Treoir before Evalle arrived. He said, "You can't be hunting nonhumans when I'm gone."

She glanced away.

Dammit, that had come out harsh, but only because he hated the idea of leaving her here alone where he couldn't protect her.

She flipped her hand, waving off his words. "Whatever."

Tristan softened his words. "I have to go, but I'll try my best to be back after the first of the year. I just don't want you getting into trouble while I'm not here to watch out for you."

That brought out cocky Mac. "Let's not forget that I'm the one who came up with this plan."

"And it almost got you killed." He lifted her over a log they'd had to cross on the way in.

Her eyes drifted down to his chest. "You're like Hercules in better packaging."

"What do you know about his *package*?"

She opened her mouth to answer and the look in her eyes shifted to one of suspicion. "Why *are* you almost naked?"

"That happens when I shift. My clothes get ripped to pieces."

"You said you'd get into trouble if you shifted to another form in this world."

He lifted a shoulder, dismissing her concern. "It's like a holding penalty in football. Only counts if you get caught."

"But in football no one gets killed for holding."

"Sometimes the risk is worth it."

She walked along silently for a moment then blurted out, "I wish you were able to stay."

"Why?" He waited to hear that she'd never met anything as strange as him, or that he might be able to help her find some nonhumans for her Kossman gig.

Dickhead brain talking again. Mac deserved better than his suspicion at this point.

She shrugged, looking self-conscious for once. "I've never met a man like you."

He jumped to what seemed the obvious conclusion to him. "You mean one who shifts into a monster and teleports?"

"I don't care about any of that. I care about the man who would not walk away from his friends or hurt me intentionally. I care about the man who makes love to me like I'm the only woman in the world. I care about the man inside you."

She *was* the only woman in his world. He should say those words, but caring about someone generally came back to bite him in the ass.

Mac laughed and told him, "I care about you even though that probably scares the crap out of you."

He cut his eyes to her and she sent a smug look back at him, adding, "But you don't scare me. Not even with those bright neon eyes. I really like them."

"You might be a half bubble off after all."

She laughed and his heart hit his chest, wanting to get closer to that sound and to her. Some might not see her as a classic beauty, but he saw what made her special and beautiful to him. His damn conscience backhanded him for not telling her that after what she'd just given him.

Tristan squeezed her hand and started to speak when a shout cut him off.

"Tristan, shake a leg," Petrina grumbled. "Let's go."

Mac picked up her pace. "She's right. I don't want you to leave, but you have to get back in time."

"That's probably not going to happen."

#

Tristan kept a hand on Mac as she strode across the parking lot to where only one vehicle waited. She suggested, "Maybe I should bring you clothes before some female jogger shows up."

"Don't like me showing off my body?" Tristan quipped, flexing his chest and arms.

"No," Mac said. That one word sounded possessive as hell, but she wanted him to know she would not be forgotten. "There are limits to my patience, and you don't want to piss me off."

Bernie jumped out of Otto's minivan and ran over to them.

Tristan swung Mac around where Bernie couldn't hear and whispered, "You're gorgeous and hot. You know that? Especially when you get your back up."

Her eyes twinkled with delight.

Points to me. I must have said the right thing this time.

Tristan continued pulling her along to the van while Bernie asked questions nonstop.

"What happened to Sethos? Is he coming back? Can we teleport ..."

Tristan ignored him until they reached the rest of the group.

Petrina stepped out. "Glad to see you could conjure up some shorts. Not that I haven't seen you shift, but there's only so much my retinas can take."

Petrina got mouthy when she worried, and she was clearly stressed but not admitting it. Tristan said, "Glad to see you, too."

He introduced everyone, then he filled the others in on what happened to Sethos.

Petrina waved off the deaths. "No great loss there."

Bernie started whining, "You need to take Petrina back, Tristan. No reason in all of us getting busted."

A lead ball of worry hit Tristan's gut. "I know."

Petrina said, "I'm not leaving you here, Bernie."

Standing tall, Bernie argued, "I didn't save you during the war on Treoir to see Macha harm you."

Bernie and Petrina squared off and started arguing.

Tristan was getting between them when Mac whistled loud enough to blow Tristan's eardrums. When he uncovered his ears, he glared at her. "What?"

"Why can't you all go back together?"

"Because I don't have that kind of power. I've never teleported between realms with more than one person at a time."

"What about that linking thing?"

Silence slammed the tense air.

Petrina asked, "What about the linking?"

Mac sounded exasperated with them. "Wouldn't that give him the power he needs to teleport *all* of you?"

Otto walked around, stroking his graying beard. Thick brown and gray hair curled to his neck, but with his glamour, he kept the pointy ears hidden. He cocked his head. "That has merit, Tristan."

Bernie and Petrina looked at Tristan. He sighed. "We've never tried it. Could be dangerous."

"More dangerous than trying to link for the first time while facing off with a crazy sorcerer?" Mac asked, sounding incredulous.

Well, hell. She did have a point, and Tristan felt pretty damn strong with the three of them still linked to him.

Petrina crossed her arms. "I agree. I'm not leaving without both of you."

Bernie beamed, as if Petrina had showered him with kisses. "Really?"

Tristan pointed at him. "Stay away from my sister."

That seemed to inspire even more hope in Bernie. "You really think I have a chance with her?"

Tristan said, "What happened to all that crap I heard about Cl–"

Bernie started waving his hands at Tristan, as if his next words were going to create a disaster.

Mac shook her head as she watched the banter, but Tristan noticed the wistful look that crossed her face. Was she actually enjoying being in the middle of this mess?

"*Her* is standing right here," Petrina told Bernie. Then she gave Tristan a warning look. "I can handle this myself. Are you going to teleport us back to Treoir or not?"

CHAPTER 12

Tristan tossed his hands up. "Okay, I agree. I'll try teleporting all three of us. Give me a minute." He walked Mac across the parking lot, now taking on a layer of sleet. He turned, blocking Mac's view of his nosy friends and sister.

He cupped her face. "I don't want to leave you—"

"—but your buddy Otto can give me a ride home and you're almost out of time. I don't want anything to happen to you."

Mac was working hard to make this easy on him.

How was he going to leave her? "I mentioned earlier that I'm stuck on Treoir until the first of the year, but I'll come back as soon as I can." *If I can.*

Her smile did a poor job of hiding the sadness in her eyes. "I understand. I'll be busy while you're gone."

Tristan didn't want her working for that guy, Kossman, but he had to give Mac space to do what she wanted.

He'd leave instructions with Otto for security.

That wouldn't fix her biggest problem. He was leaving her and she had nothing to give Kossman. In her shoes, he'd be throwing trees around at this point. "Are you still going to work with Kossman?"

"If he'll keep me. He might give me another chance, since Seth obviously won't be showing up for work. Look, I'm leaving first just so you don't get to leave me twice."

That gave his heart a cramp.

Tristan walked Mac back to the van, turning her into his arms for one last kiss to let her know he was serious about returning. When he lifted his head, she grinned and said, "Hold that thought."

Mac would be fine.

Once he had her settled inside the van, he asked Otto for an extra phone. Otto pulled out one of five that were in his console and handed it to Tristan.

"Thanks, Otto. I'll be in touch when I get back."

Otto nodded and backed out, then drove away.

Bernie asked, "What's the phone for? It won't work on Treoir."

Tristan thumbed keys with blinding speed, ignoring Bernie.

Petrina told Bernie, "He's sending a message he didn't want us to hear."

"Oh."

"Dollar waiting on a dime, Tristan," Petrina ragged. "We have six minutes to make it back before Evalle shows, and I have no idea how much time we lose teleporting."

Tristan hit send, shoved the phone in his pocket, and nodded. Teleporting all three would either work, or they wouldn't have to deal with Macha. "Both of you focus your energy on me."

Bernie suggested, "Let's hold hands. Contact has to be good, right?"

Tristan gave him an appalled look.

Petrina grabbed Bernie's hand and snapped at Tristan, "You aren't going to lose your man card, dammit. Bernie, grab Tristan's arm." She latched onto Tristan, too.

He closed his mind to everything except getting them out of there.

Colors swirled in his mind, then Mac's smiling face came into view. He might get used to holidays after all.

"Wipe that stupid look off your face, Tristan," Petrina hissed.

He opened his eyes, and they were standing at the edge of the woods he'd envisioned for their arrival.

Evalle called out, "Tristan? Is that you?"

"Yeah."

She came walking quickly across a football-field-size lawn that spread even further in front of Treoir Castle.

He whispered, "We did it."

"I know." Petrina and Bernie were laughing like kids.

It must have been contagious, because Tristan started chuckling.

By the time Evalle reached them, Tristan had managed to pull himself under control and cross his arms. If he sounded like anything other than his normal, surly self, she'd be suspicious. He scowled at her. "What? We don't have enough to do, and now damn meetings?"

Evalle slowed then paused her step. Her black hair was back in its usual ponytail. She had on her vintage BDU shirt and faded jeans. Those boots concealed fighting blades, which she shouldn't need here.

Evalle lifted an eyebrow at Petrina and Bernie.

Tristan glanced over, and they looked like two minions imitating him with crossed arms and serious mugs.

He was too tired for all of this. "Why are you here, Evalle? Thought you and your tomcat were holed up in Atlanta."

Her gaze shifted to him. "We're remodeling a new building and hope to move in by the first of the year. But the reason I'm here is because the Tribunal put off the vote. I don't feel right staying in Atlanta while you're all stuck here. I'm doing everything I can to get our petition approved. In the meantime, we'll spend the holidays together."

Tristan started to mouth off at her, then changed his mind and said, "Thank you."

Evalle's head snapped back. "Are you sick?"

He smiled. "Just in the holiday mood."

CHAPTER 13

Mac nodded as she listened to Kossman, holding the phone to her ear on her way to the kitchen. It was good to be home. "Thank you for the position. I'm sorry the bounty call didn't work out."

"I'm just glad you weren't with Brewster when someone hit the van."

She didn't want to remember that again. "I'm glad they were both okay after the accident. I *am* surprised to hear about Seth not returning. That's ... shocking." She rolled her eyes.

"Just shows his lack of commitment. His family had some excuse about needing him in their European operations."

I bet. And that family would be one of the first groups Mac investigated.

Kossman added, "I'm not sure Seth really believed in my project, but you do, correct?"

"Absolutely." Her sincerity should have been easy to hear, since she *did* believe. And now she would have to find out what Kossman had seen at one time in his life. "Too bad for Seth, but I'm happy to benefit from his poor decision. I'm definitely in."

"And you say the bounty call was only a ploy for the money? No glowing eyes?"

"Sorry, sir, but that woman had no integrity." Mac did not feel guilty about letting Kossman think Bernie's ex-girlfriend, who'd tried to sell him, had lied. "As for the eyes, no, the man I saw at that house did not have glowing eyes." Truth. Tristan's eyes had been normal at that time.

"I hope the gentleman contacts me so I can make amends. I've got to revamp our team's protocols. I don't want innocent humans terrorized. You'll be a big help with that. I owe you more than the bonus you received."

"I'm very pleased with that bonus and to have my job, Mr. Kossman. I'm celebrating by buying a Christmas tree this weekend." And a security system for Miss Wilma's house. The bonus had been generous, and protecting Miss Wilma and her home was the first proactive step Mac was taking to stop Brandon's interference in her life and the lives of people she cared about.

"That reminds me ... I'm sending you something."

"What?"

"It's a surprise. Enjoy. See you Monday."

She ended the call and watched the rain now pouring down. The temperature was high enough it wouldn't freeze, but the cold wet was so nasty she did not look forward to bundling up and leaving this nice warm fireplace. "I *am* getting Miss Wilma a tree today. End of discussion and excuses."

Good time to do it while Miss Wilma and her Dachshund were sound asleep upstairs. That would give Mac time to drag the tree in, set it up, and get the basic trimming and lights in place.

Someone tapped at the back door.

Mac wondered who would come to the back, and tiptoed there cautiously. When she moved the curtain aside to expose the windowpanes, a young man with a nice smile stood there.

He asked, "Are you Miss Mackenzie?"

"Yes."

"I have a delivery for you."

She stretched her neck to see what he had, and a green fir tree came into view.

Mr. Kossman's surprise! Mac had expected one of those stacked gift box towers full of edible goodies.

This was way better.

She opened the door and stepped back. "Please come in. I'm so excited."

He smiled brightly, hoisted the tree as if it weighed nothing, and walked in.

She watched him, thinking about the people she'd met with extraordinary power, but then shook her head, muttering, "He's just a young, strong delivery boy."

He turned to her as he reached the living room. "I see a spot next to the window. Will that work?"

"Yes. I moved everything for the tree."

"If you'll wait just a moment, it will be a nicer surprise once I set it up."

"Okay. Go ahead."

She walked over to rinse the glass she'd just drunk eggnog from, then she turned to offer the young man a glass, but he walked back in as if he had finished. She asked, "Did it fit?"

"Yes, ma'am. I'll be going now."

"Wow, you have it set up already?" How had he done that so quickly? "Wait, let me grab my purse."

"Oh, no, ma'am. My uncle Otto would have my hide if I took money from you."

Her jaw dropped.

When he walked past, she saw pointy tips on his ears, sticking out of his thick, wavy brown hair.

She ran into the living room, and the tree was trimmed with glowing strings of old-fashioned, multicolored lights.

How did he do that so quickly?

One round copper ornament hung close to the bottom. She squatted and turned it toward the light to see a circle enclosing the shape of a gryphon with green eyes.

Words engraved around the bottom said, *Until next time, T.*

The End

Dear reader:

Hope you enjoyed this short novel and its unusual story world. Tristan is one of the characters from my Belador urban fantasy series, and if you read that series, you'll see him again, as well as Mac.

Evalle Kincaid and her Skinwalker, Storm, who shifts into a black jaguar, will return in ROGUE BELADOR, book 7 coming out April 2016. Tzader Burke and Vladimir Quinn are primary characters in the series as well. Their adventures will be in upcoming books. If you enjoy urban fantasy with plenty of action and romance, I invite you to give the Belador series a try.

And, of course, Evalle's adorable pet gargoyle Feenix will be back.

Happy Reading!

~~Dianna Love

To contact Dianna –

Website: www.AuthorDiannaLove.com and www.Beladors.com

Facebook – Author Dianna Love

Twitter @DiannaLove

Dianna Love Street Team Facebook group page (Readers invited)

Newsletter (sign up to stay current on all of Dianna's events) at www.AuthorDiannaLove.com

REVIEWS ON BELADOR BOOKS:

"…non-stop tense action, filled with twists, betrayals, danger, and a beautiful sensual romance. As always with Dianna Love, I was on the edge of my seat, unable to pull myself away."
~~Barb, The Reading Cafe

"…shocking developments and a whopper of an ending... and I may have exclaimed aloud more than once…Bottom line: I really kind of loved it."
 ~~Jen, top 500 Reviewer

"DEMON STORM leaves you breathless on countless occasions."
~~Amelia Richard, SingleTitles

"...Its been a very long time since I've felt this passionate about getting the next installment in a series. Even J. K. Rowling's Harry Potter books."
~~Bryonna Nobles, Demons, Dreams and Dragon Wings

Belador novels are released in print, e-book and audio.

BLOOD TRINITY – Belador Book 1

Atlanta has become the battlefield between human and demon.

As an outcast among her own people, Evalle Kincaid has walked the line between human and beast her whole life as a half-blood Belador. An Alterant. Her true origins unknown, she searches to learn more about her past before it kills her, but when a demon claims a young woman in a terrifying attack and there's no one else to blame, Evalle comes under suspicion.

The one person who can help her is Storm, the sexy new agent brought in to catch her in a lie, just one of his gifts besides being a Skinwalker. On a deadly quest for her own survival, Evalle is forced to work with the mysterious stranger who has the power to unravel her world. Through the sordid underbelly of an alternate Atlanta where nothing is as it seems to the front lines of the city where former allies now hunt her, Evalle must prove her innocence or pay the ultimate price. But saving herself is the least of her problems if she doesn't stop the coming apocalypse. The clock is ticking and Atlanta is about to ignite.

"BLOOD TRINITY is an ingenious urban fantasy ... Book One in the Belador series will enthrall you during every compellingly entertaining scene." **Amelia Richards, Single Titles**

"...a well written book that will take you out of your everyday life and transport you to an exciting new world..." **Heated Steve**

~*~

ALTERANT: Belador Book 2

Evalle must hunt her own kind...or die with them.

In this explosive new world of betrayals and shaky alliances, as the only Alterant not incarcerated, Evalle faces an impossible task -- recapture three dangerous, escaped creatures before they slaughter more humans...or her.

When words uttered in the heat of combat are twisted against her, Evalle is blamed for the prison break of three dangerous Alterants and forced to recapture the escapees. Deals with gods and goddesses are tricky at best, and now the lives of all Beladors, and the safety of innocent humans, rides on Evalle's success. Her Skinwalker partner, Storm, is determined to plant all four of his black jaguar paws in the middle of her world, but Evalle has no time for a love life. Not present when a Tribunal sends her to the last place she wants to show her face.

The only person she can ask for help is the one man who wants to see her dead.

"There are SO many things in this series that I want to learn more about; there's no way I could list them all." **Lily, Romance Junkies Reviews**

~*~

THE CURSE: Belador book 3

Troll powered gang wars explode in cemeteries and no one in Atlanta is safe.

Demonic Svart Trolls have invaded Atlanta and Evalle suddenly has little hope of fulfilling a promise with the freedom of an entire race hanging in the balance, even if she had more than two days. She takes a leap of faith, seeking help from Isak, the Black Ops specialist who recently put Evalle in his cross hairs and has a personal vendetta against Alterants who killed his best friend.

Bloody troll led gang wars force Evalle into unwittingly exposing a secret that endangers all she holds dear, and complicates her already tumultuous love life with the mysterious Skinwalker, Storm. But it's when the entire Medb coven comes after her that Evalle is forced to make a game-changing decision with no time left on the clock.

"Evalle, continues to be one of my favorite female warriors in paranormal/urban fantasy... I loved The Curse... This was a great story from start to finish, super fun, lots of action, couples to root for, and a fantastic heroine." **Barb, The Reading Café**

~*~

RISE OF THE GRYPHON: Belador Book 4

If dying is the cost of protecting those you love... bring it.

Evalle has a chance to find out her true origin, and give all Alterants a place in the world. To do so, she'll have to take down the Belador traitor and bring home a captured friend, which means infiltrating the dangerous Medb coven. To do that, she'll have to turn her back on her vows and enter a vicious game to the death. What she does discover about Alterants is not good, especially for the Beladors.

Her best friends, Tzader and Quinn, face unthinkable choices, as relationships with the women they love grow twisted. With time ticking down on a decision that will compel allies to become deadly enemies, Evalle turns to Storm and takes a major step in their relationship, but the witchdoctor he's been hunting now stalks Evalle. Now Evalle is forced to embrace her destiny . . . but at what price?

"Longtime fans of the Belador series will have much to celebrate in the fearless Evalle Kincaid's fourth outing...with such heart and investment, each scene has an intensity that will quicken the pulse and capture the imagination..."
— RT Book Reviews

~*~

DEMON STORM: Belador book 5

We all have demons... some are more real than others.

With Treoir Island in shambles after a Medb attack that left the survival of the missing Belador warrior queen in question and Belador powers compromised, there is one hope for her return and their future – Evalle Kincaid, whose recent transformation has turned her into an even more formidable warrior. First she has to locate Storm, the Skinwalker she's bonded with who she believes can find the Belador queen, but Storm stalks the witch doctor who's threatening Evalle's life. When he finally corners the witch doctor, she throws Storm a curve that may cost him everything, including Evalle. The hunter becomes the hunted, and Evalle must face her greatest nightmare to save Storm and the Beladors or watch the future of mankind fall to deadly preternatural predators.

DEMON STORM includes a BONUS SHORT STORY - DEADLY FIXATION, from the Belador world.

"There is so much action in this book I feel like I've burned calories just reading it."
D Antonio

"...nonstop adventures overflowing with danger and heartfelt emotions. DEMON STORM leaves you breathless on countless occasions."
~~Amelia Richard, Single Titles

~*~

WITCHLOCK: Belador Book 6

Witchlock vanished in the 13th century ... or did it?

If Atlanta falls, Witchlock will sweep the country in a bloodbath.
After finally earning her place among the Beladors, Evalle is navigating the ups and downs of her new life with Storm when she's sucked into a power play between her Belador tribe and the Medb coven. Both groups claim possession of the Alterant gryphons, especially Evalle, the gryphon leader. But an influx of demons and dark witches into Atlanta threatens to unleash war between covens, pitting allies against each other as a legendary majik known as Witchlock invades the city and attacks powerful beings. Evalle has one hope for stopping the invasion, but the cost may be her sanity and having to choose which friend to save.

"Evalle and friends are back in another high energy, pulse pounding adventure...Fans of Rachel Caine's Weather Warden series will enjoy this series. I surely do." **In My Humble Opinion Blogspot**

~*~

ROGUE BELADOR: Belador Book 7 (April 2016)

Immortals fear little ... except a secret in the wrong hands.

While searching for a way to save Brina of Treoir's failing memories, Tzader Burke discovers someone who can help her if Tzader is willing to sneak into the heart of his enemy's stronghold—TÅµr Medb. He'll do anything to protect the woman he loves from becoming a mindless empty shell, but his decision could be the catalyst for an apocalyptic war. The deeper he digs for the truth, the more lies he uncovers that shake the very foundation of being a Belador and the future of his clan.

Tzader's ready to execute his mission. Alone. But the minute his best friends Quinn and Evalle, plus her Skinwalker mate Storm, find out about his suicidal plan they organize a black ops team around him. While battling on every front, one secret surfaces that two immortal powers have spent thousands of years keeping buried. Tzader and his team have no choice but to fight for what they believe in, because the world as they know it is never going to be the same again.

~*~

Now is a great time to jump into the Belador world and find out why millions love this urban fantasy series.

To keep up on these books, join Dianna Love's newsletter at
www.AuthorDiannaLove.com

Haunted Memories: From the Belador world

I stared up at the menacing gargoyle carved into the corner of a mausoleum in Atlanta's Oakland Cemetery and questioned my IQ level. My last visit to a cemetery at night had left emotional scars that stayed with me for years.

Agreeing to a stupid bet with Vivian, my manipulative older sister, cost me a few intelligence points. At nineteen, I shouldn't allow emotions to get the best of me.

Neither should I be terrified of cemeteries, but that fear had been earned honestly.

"What are you waiting on, Chelsea? Put the sack over your head."

I glared at Vivian and her smarmy boyfriend, Sonny.

Vivian ragged on me for having no boyfriend, but hers was no prize. Her pack of eight friends that ranged from nineteen to twenty-three was present to witness my humiliation. Not a friendly face among them.

One of the girls started clucking like a chicken.

Another one called out, "Just admit you're afraid and accept defeat."

I couldn't. I'd never live it down after betting my sister the use of her new car, a badass corvette, for a month. It would kill her to hand the keys over, which was how she'd sucked me in.

Of course, if I lost, I'd have to clean her apartment weekly for a month.

Swallowing, I took a breath. As a child, I'd gotten lost during a night tour in a New Orleans cemetery. When I thought I saw a ghost, I'd raced away screaming bloody murder.

This was a mistake.

"Never mind. You can't do it," Vivian snapped, dismissing me.

Oh, hell no. I lifted the black bag and yanked it down over my head.

That brought on the jeering and laughter.

Someone tied my wrists in front of me. My heart jumped around like it wanted to get out and run a hundred yard dash.

A strap dropped across the back of my neck. Then the camera for filming my terror was placed in my hands.

Sonny's nasally voice ordered, "Hold this straight out. Keep the strap taut and it will film you plus a couple feet on each side. It's my dad's so don't bang it against anything."

I murmured, "I'll try not to, but I have to run into things to find my way."

"Bang up your knuckles, twit. Not the camera."

Sonny and Vivian were a perfect, coldblooded pair.

My breathing picked up. I fought the urge to panic. Not in front of this bunch or I'd lose before I got started. Sure, I was scared, but I wanted to see Vivian hand over the keys to her precious car.

I'd been in this cemetery before, but in daylight. All those rumors about spirits showing up at night couldn't be true. Right?

Icy fingers wrapped around my upper arm. Vivian whispered, "Feel free to cry or scream at any time to end this. I'll send Sonny for you."

That terrified me more than potential ghosts. "I'm doing this."

I sounded confident. Amazing what I could do when working on a high dose of emotionally driven insanity.

I started forward and had made twenty steps when my hands bumped into something hard. Ouch. A headstone or a statue?

Laughter erupted far behind me and Sonny shouted, "Careful, twit."

If not for fear of retribution, I'd scar up his camera just so he'd have to explain to his dad. I kept walking, turning left then right after each obstacle to hopefully continue toward a new guy in the group, Ed, who waited at the other end.

Something brushed across my arm and I jerked, but managed not to scream. Heart pounding, I stood still. Wind stirred and this time I recognized the next brief touch as a leafy branch.

Breathe. Okay, I had this. *Just back away slowly and walk around it.* But as I went to take a step, the air turned chilly and thick fingers gently cupped my upper arm. I couldn't squeeze out a sound.

A smooth voice that sounded like Morgan Freeman playing the role of an old Southern man chided, "Don't worry none. I'm not gonna hurt ya. I don't like those idiots bein' mean to you."

My heartbeat hammered faster, but he hadn't sounded dangerous. Would Vivian even care if someone attacked me in here?

"Come on now. We gonna get you to the end where you can show them you got grit."

Sounded good, but could I trust him? "Who are you?"

"Just someone who don't like mean people."

While I made up my mind on the old guy, he tugged me forward, then gently pulled me side-to-side, guiding me in what seemed like the right direction as he gave encouragement. "You doin' good."

"Thank you." I debated calling this off right now, but what if he was just a Good Samaritan? Plus, the camera had to be filming him.

Something about his voice soothed my fears. Still, this was too risky. I prepared for defeat when I heard Ed call out, "This way, Chelsea."

The old guy said, "See? You're almost through. Keep goin' ten steps and you'll be done."

He released my arm. I said, "Wait. What's your name?"

"I'm called Grady."

"Do you live here?"

"I stay near Grady Hospital. You go on now, and don't let that nasty sister of yours mess with you again."

"I won't. Thank you."

"You're welcome."

I kept walking forward until Ed said, "Whoa, hot shot."

He pulled the sack off my head. I looked around for Grady while Ed texted the group that I'd won the bet. While we waited for everyone to arrive, Ed replayed the video.

I stared at each frame, right to the end when Ed stepped up next to me on the same side where Grady had walked.

There was no one on camera except me, carrying on a one-sided conversation.

Ed shocked me by brushing a strand of hair behind my ear. "Good job, Chelsea, but who were you talking to?"

~*~

Grady is a Nightstalker in the Belador series. Nightstalkers are ghouls that will trade intel (ghoul informants) about the supernatural world for a handshake with a powerful being. That quick handshake allows the Nightstalker to take corporeal form for ten minutes. Grady is special because he once had an extra long handshake and can occasionally turn solid for brief periods on his own.

Please visit **www.AuthorDiannaLove.com** to find out more about the Beladors and all of Dianna's books. And I always appreciate reviews.

www.BELADORS.com